How To Seduce The Ex

The How To Series

Mallory Black

Itty Bitty Creative LLC

THE HOW TO SERIES

Mallory Black

HOW TO SEDUCE THE EX
Written by Mallory Black

This book is an original publication by Mallory Black.

Cover Design by: Rachel Connolly
Edited by: G. G. Royale
Proofread by: Julie Barney

ISBN: 978-1-959065-09-8

PRAISE FOR *HOW TO ONE-NIGHT STAND*

"Nailed it!! I couldn't put it down. This book gives you all of the feel good that you want to read in a romance novel."

"You'll get all the feels, some angst, some intense moments, and of course there's spicy sizzle. Ms. Black dials in perfectly to today's "one and done" dating scene."

"I couldn't put it down. It's an absolute must read! It's got everything. Office romance, age gap, comedy, and sexiness."

"5 stars and many more. I would definitely recommend it to all. It's a wonderful, hot and steamy debut. Most definitely worth reading."

PRAISE FOR *HOW TO FAKE A FIANCÉ*

"A smexy romance with such heart!"

"I loved this book. There is nothing more perfect than a determined, compassionate, sexy man who isn't afraid to follow a connection to another's heart!"

"Fantastic! I enjoyed this book so much. It was such a delight to read. The story was fun and also emotional with great romance!"

ABOUT *HOW TO SEDUCE THE EX*

I've tried to move on. He's making sure I can't.

Lyla

I auditioned for the show on a whim. I figured...it's a free vacation. What's the worst that could happen?

Imagine my surprise when I arrive and I'm told I'm a cast member on The One That Got Away—a show built around reconnecting with your ex.

And mine just walked into the villa.

Scott Bennett. The boy I never got over, and the man I never forgave.

He's got the same broad shoulders, the same smug smirk, and judging by the look in his eyes? He doesn't plan to leave here without me.

Scott

She thought she could move on? On national television? Cute.

The second I found out she auditioned, I made sure I got cast, too. Now we're under the same roof, cameras rolling, and guys are lining up to "get to know her."

They can try.

She was mine before the spotlight. And if I have anything to do with it, she'll be mine after.

I lost her once. I won't make that mistake twice.

Chapter One

Dallas, Texas

Lyla

The bustle emergency hits at 2:47p.m.

Hanging tulle from on of the aisle markers snags around my heel as I pivot across the marble floor, barely catching myself before I plow into a six-foot arrangement of imported peonies on a center table ahead. I steady the vase with one hand, juggle my coffee with the other, and keep moving.

"Lyla, please hurry." The voice of Kiera Young—soon to be Knight—shakes through my phone. "The bustle just ripped. There's fabric everywhere—"

"I'm coming. Thirty seconds." I don't slow down. "Breathe. You're fine."

She isn't fine. But that's why I'm here.

I push through the bridal-suite doors with my emergency kit in the inseam pocket of my dress. Kiera stands in the center of the room in her Vera Wang gown, frozen in horror. Pearls and thread scatter at her feet like evidence at a crime scene. Her maid of honor and bestie, Kami Hernandez, is holding torn fabric in both hands like it might bite her.

"It's ruined," Kiera whispers.

"It's not." I drop to my knees, fingers already assessing the damage. "Kami, steamer. Now. Kiera, I need you to trust me."

Trust.

That's a word I use professionally at least fifty times a week. Brides trust me with the biggest day of their lives. Vendors trust my contracts. Venues trust my timelines.

I rebuild broken things for a living.

"Fifteen minutes," I say calmly, threading a needle. "You'll walk down that aisle flawless."

My voice never wavers. My hands never shake. The chaos around me quiets because I don't give it permission to stay loud.

Seven years of building Clark Events from nothing has trained me well. I don't panic. I problem solve.

Fifteen minutes later, Kiera glides toward the altar like nothing ever happened. Jonathan Knight's face softens when he sees her. The room fades for them. They look at each other like the rest of the world doesn't exist.

My chest tightens for half a second.

I swallow it down.

I orchestrate fairy tales. I don't live inside them.

By the time the ceremony ends, my feet ache and my coffee is cold. I finally check my phone.

One new message.

> Katie.

I open it expecting a vendor question.

Instead:

> I can't do this anymore. The stress is affecting my relationship. I need something more stable. I'm sorry.

There's no notice. No warning. Just a clean exit.

I stare at the screen as the reception swells behind me—champagne popping, laughter rising, string quartet shifting into something upbeat.

Four hundred guests tomorrow for the Beckman wedding. A budget that rivals the revenue of small countries.

And now I'm alone.

I close my eyes briefly.

Control.

I handle it. I always handle it.

I text back something professional. Something gracious. Something I don't feel.

Then I slide my phone into my clutch and walk back into the ballroom with a smile so seamless no one notices it's glued on.

Two hours later, I find my bestie, Quinn, by the bar, glowing in a way that only women freshly in love do. Nathan Knight, Jonathan's brother, has his arm around her waist, his thumb tracing lazy circles over her hip.

Easy. Comfortable. Certain.

"There she is," Quinn says, pulling me into a hug. "I heard about the bustle incident."

"Just another Saturday." I accept the champagne she hands me. "You two are disgustingly happy."

Nathan grins. "We aim to offend."

They laugh together. Effortless.

I watch them for a second longer than I mean to.

After everything they survived—the public fallout, the separation—they chose each other again. Not because it was convenient. Because it was worth the fight.

"I'm glad I had front-row seats to the epic romance," I say lightly.

Quinn bumps her shoulder against mine. "You'll get yours."

I smile in the exact way I've perfected for these moments.

"Sure."

My phone vibrates again.

I almost ignore it, but habit wins.

. . .

Apex Entertainment

Subject: Congratulations, Lyla!

My stomach drops.

Congratulations. After reviewing thousands of applications, we are thrilled to offer you a spot on Paradise Found. Filming begins in two weeks…

Ten days. One hundred thousand dollars. National exposure.

The ballroom noise fades into a distant hum.

Breathing feels strange for a second.

Quinn leans over. “Is that what I think it is?”

“I applied months ago,” I admit quietly. “It was three in the morning. I was exhausted. It felt reckless.” I swallow. “They want me.”

Her eyes widen. “That’s incredible.”

It is. But it’s also terrifying.

The prize money would wipe out my remaining business loan. I could hire a full-time assistant. Expand. Stop operating in survival mode.

And if I’m being honest with myself, part of me is tired of endless dates that feel like interviews for a job neither of us really wants.

Maybe controlled chaos in paradise is easier than swiping through strangers.

Before I can think further, Nathan’s phone buzzes.

He glances down, frowning.

“Huh.”

“What?” Quinn asks.

“Our head of security just requested leave. Ten days.” He shrugs. “That’s rare.”

Something tightens in my stomach.

“Who?” I ask, keeping my voice neutral.

"Scott Bennett," Nathan replies. "Former Marine. Hasn't taken a day off once since he's started working for us four months ago."

The champagne turns to ice in my throat.

Scott Bennett.

The name hits like pressure shifting too fast in my ears.

Ten years collapse inward.

The last time I saw him, he was eighteen and promising me forever with his mouth on mine.

Then he was gone.

No fight. No goodbye. Just silence so complete it made me question whether any of it had been real.

And the whole time he was working for the Knights?

"Lyla?" Quinn asks softly.

"I-I'm fine," I stammer through my lie.

I'm very much not fine.

Scott taking leave the same amount of time I'll be gone?

It's a coincidence. It has to be.

People don't rearrange their lives for ghosts.

Later that night, I sit in my apartment with the acceptance email open on my laptop.

The glow from the screen washes the room in blue light. The city outside my window hums, distant and indifferent.

Paradise Found.

Tropical beaches. Curated romance. A fish bowl of an environment where everyone brings out their inner TV personality for money and fifteen minutes.

It's almost laughable.

My dating history could be summarized as a promising start, slow unravel, then quiet disappointment.

The only exception is the one man who didn't unravel.

He detonated.

I close my eyes and let the memory surface, just once.

His truck parked by the lake. The smell of gasoline and summer air. His hands always warm, always sure. The way he used to say my name like it belonged to him.

And then—nothing. Silence.

I spent months wondering what I did wrong. Replaying every conversation. Every touch.

Eventually the exhaustion won.

You can only bleed over a ghost for so long before you build scar tissue. I built a business instead.

Structure. Contracts. Clear expectations. Predictable outcomes.

Love isn't predictable. But money is. Exposure is. *Paradise Found* is leverage.

That's all it is.

I click Reply. I accept.

The second I send it, a strange calm settles in my chest.

This is strategic. Smart. And most definitely not about him.

I shut the laptop and walk to my bedroom, shedding my blazer, my heels, the perfectly composed wedding planner persona.

In the mirror, my reflection looks steady. Controlled. Competent. Not like a woman who still feels a flicker of something at the sound of a name she hasn't spoken in a decade.

"Please let it be coincidence," I murmur to the empty room.

Because if it's not... If he knew... If he's anywhere near this... I don't know what version of myself he'll meet.

The girl he left behind doesn't exist anymore. And the woman standing here doesn't break easily.

I climb into bed and turn off the light.

Ten days in paradise. Ten days under cameras. Ten days that could help my business in the long run.

It's opportunity. It's exposure. It's controlled risk. It has nothing to do with Scott Bennett. I repeat that to myself until sleep takes me. And I don't dream.

Scott

The Bennett estate gates groan open as I pull through, the sound dragging up the long drive like the house itself is clearing its throat to remind me who used to own me.

I park directly in front of the main entrance—something that would've set my father off—and kill the engine. The mansion I've been avoiding for the four months since I've been back looms ahead, all columns and quiet judgment. Every window stares like an accusing eye.

I'm not here to reminisce.

Fuck no.

The final estate paperwork waits in his study. Signatures, transfer documents, legal loose ends—clean cuts through a life I never asked for. The last threads of a fortune and business I'm shocked I even inherited and certainly didn't earn in the eyes of my father, but I'll damn well use.

I step out of the truck. Cold air bites my lungs, sharp as a blade. The driveway crunches beneath my boots.

The house smells the same when I push inside—polish and old wood, laced with something stale, like control seeped into the walls. It's quiet. Too quiet.

He's been dead for months, and I still feel him here, a ghost in the bones of this place.

The hall echoes as I walk, my footsteps steady. My body knows this house. Every corner. Every blind spot. Every place a boy learned to stay silent.

When I reach the study, the room looks exactly how I remember it. Heavy desk. Leather chair. Neatly stacked files, as if he planned to come back. The portrait above the fireplace stares down, his face carved in oil—cold power, a man who believed to be loved was to be feared.

I drop the folder onto the desk and exhale through my nose.

Ten years in the Marines burned away a lot. The flinch. The doubt. But not all of it. Not the part of me that still aches for her.

Lyla.

Her name strikes me like light a bolt of lightning, sharp and immediate. I don't say it out loud. I don't need to.

I haven't seen her in ten years, and I still remember everything about her—her laugh, her mouth, her long pale curls, the way she climbed into my lap like it was as natural as breathing. The heat of her skin against mine, the way she looked at me like I was her rock. Something worth fighting for.

Every deployment. Every bunker. Every night staring at a ceiling in some hellhole, telling myself I'd come back stronger. Worthy. Able to stand before my father without breaking.

And with bits of my paychecks over the years, I bought a small house when I was overseas, hoping—promising to myself—when I could return, we'd spend our lives together there.

Half a year in boot camp and SOI training, then several deployments all over the world. I did anything and everything to avoid being found by my father's people. And I've carried that choice for a decade.

Then after about nine-and-a-half years, I found out the bastard croaked. I didn't go to the asshole's funeral. Didn't give a shit what my parent's "friends" thought or would gossip about. Especially when they were the ones who pretended to not have known his behavior toward me from the time I was a kid.

Fuck them.

Instead, I requested an early honorable discharge that same day. I got out two months later and immediately flew out on the red-eye to Dallas. Wanting to build a life outside of my family, I got myself a job at Knight Industries as their head of security and a small apartment for rent that's only a few blocks from Lyla's apartment complex.

I came back to claim what was mine—my name, my life, my future.

And still...

None of it matters. None of that compares to the one thing I truly want back.

I drag my folder closer and start sorting. Paperwork. Titles. Estates. Debts. Despite the busy work, it's nothing more than a distraction. Because the moment I stop, the same thought crashes in, uninvited and relentless.

Where is she doing now?

Despite being overseas, I'd found ways to keep quiet tabs on her and at least know what she was up to. No way for my father to find out, in case he was still watching her, waiting to see if I'd make contact.

But I quickly discovered I could do much more for her once I was back in Dallas and my old man died. Nothing that she'd notice. Nothing that would touch her life directly.

Her apartment building's security was shit—outdated camera, dim lighting. One anonymous call fixed that. New system. Better locks. And none of it could lead back to me.

When a vendor tried to screw her business, doors opened elsewhere. A "friend of the company" stepped in. Terms shifted. The asshole folded.

When a big client wavered, the booking stabilized. A payment cleared that shouldn't have. The right strings were pulled.

Everything I did, and continue to do in the shadows, is to keep her world turning. To keep her safe.

Because even from a distance, she's mine to protect.

She doesn't know. She doesn't need to. I just need her safe.

Most would call me obsessed. I call it restraint.

My phone vibrates across the desk, the insistent vibration, yanking me back into the present and slicing through the quiet focus of the office like an unwelcome intrusion. I glance at the screen and see a number I don't recognize glaring back at me in bold white text. For a moment, I consider letting it go to voicemail, but after the third ring, something nudges me to answer—curiosity, boredom, or maybe just the need for a break from the seemingly endless reports on the table. I swipe to accept the call.

"Bennett," I say, keeping my tone clipped and professional, already half-expecting a telemarketer or some distant relative coming out of the woodwork chasing family ties.

"Scott Bennett?" The voice on the line hesitates, laced with a nervous tremor that rings faintly familiar, though I can't pin it down right away.

"Yeah. Who is this?"

A quick, awkward laugh filters through. "It's Alex Davis—from high school. You might not remember me all that well; I was the one always buried in my Nintendo Switch, barely looking up from a Pokémon battle during lunch."

The memory sharpens into focus: curly hair flopping over his fore-head, that perpetual glow from the handheld screen lighting his face in the cafeteria shadows. He was quiet, unassuming, but yeah—I remember him now. "Alex. Long time. What's going on?"

He exhales audibly, as if gathering courage. "Right to business; I like that. So I'm in casting these days, working for Apex Entertainment. We're putting the final touches on contestants for our new dating show —*Paradise Found*."

Dating show. The phrase hangs there, absurd and irrelevant to my world of security protocols and estate management. My thumb itches toward the End Call button, ready to politely, but quickly, dismiss this blast from the past and get back to the mountain of work that's consumed me since my old man's death—the endless days at Knight Industries as head of security, the tangled inheritance of the family estate, and stepping into the void he left in his business empire.

But Alex barrels on before I can disconnect. "One of our contestants is someone you know, back from high school."

Great, but...what does this have to do with me?

High school was several lifetimes ago. So unless he's reminiscing, I struggle to understand why he's calling me. And someone I know could be any number of forgotten faces. I pause, more out of politeness than interest, my hand still hovering near the phone. "Who?"

"Lyla Clark."

Her name crashes over me like a rogue wave—cold, forceful, knocking the air from my lungs in a single, brutal instant. For a frozen second, the world narrows to that sound, echoing in my chest. Heat flares through my veins, a savage burn that races down my spine and settles low in my gut, twisting into something feral and unforgiving. Surprise hits first, sharp as a blade, followed by a shockwave of regret and a raw, aching need. Lyla. The one I've been circling in my mind for months, ever since Dad's funeral stripped away the excuses and left me raw with the urge to physically be with her again, to explain the mess of ten years ago. But life piled on: the relentless demands of my work with the Knights, the estates' legal quagmire, the business I never wanted but couldn't abandon. And beneath it all, the coward's fear. That if I showed up now, she'd slam the door in my face, her eyes full of the hurt I'd inflicted when I vanished without a trace.

She's on a dating show.

The realization weaves through the chaos in my head. Time is slipping away—faster than I realized. For all I know, she's there to find someone else, to build a connection with a stranger who won't carry my ghosts. The thought ignites a fresh surge of panic, hot and possessive, clawing at the eyes of my control. The time I have now could be my last chance to win her back or, at least, lay bare the truth of why I left before she leaves for production and moves on for good.

But a darker thread weaves through my brain. Alex's call feels too pointed, too convenient. He knew us back then. He would've seen how inseparable we were, how the air between us always crackled.

"Why are you calling me about this?" I ask, voice low and edged. "It's not like I can do anything about it."

"That's not...entirely true."

"How so?"

He pauses long enough that I can practically hear his nerves fraying. "I shouldn't be telling you this."

"Telling me what?"

Another pause, heavier this time.

"Alex," I say, sharper now, "you called me for a reason. And I'm pretty sure it wasn't just to give me a play-by-play of what Lyla's doing on your show."

I hear him exhale deeply on the other end. "If I tell you, this conversation didn't happen."

That serious, huh?

My grip tightens on the phone. "Done. Just tell me."

"I'm so getting fired for this," he mutters. "You're not supposed to know this until day one of filming, but the show isn't for singles; it's not even called *Paradise Found*. It's another season of *The One That Got Away*. You know it?"

"Not really."

"Basically, it's the same structure of a regular dating show, but the whole thing revolves around a group of people reconnecting with their most significant exes. None of the contestants we've selected have any idea this is happening."

The words detonate in slow motion. My pulse slams in my throat. Every muscle locks as the full picture snaps into focus. Lyla, on cable television, will be facing a significant ex from her past. And given this entire conversation...

It's me.

The room tilts. My grip tightens on the phone, knuckles paling, every muscle coiled like I'm bracing for impact. I ghosted her. I disappeared without explanation. I don't deserve her—not after everything. But damn if this doesn't feel like fate shoving me toward the edge, daring me to jump.

I stare at my father's portrait like it might laugh. Choice. That's what he's offering.

The line hums with silence. Alex waits.

A sane man would say no. A sane man wouldn't walk in front of cameras and manufactured drama just for one woman. But I haven't been sane, where Lyla is concerned, since I was eighteen.

"When does filming start?"

He hesitates only a second. "First day of shooting is in two weeks."

I have fourteen days, maybe less, to decide whether I'm going to walk into a televised ambush, hand over every private wound we ever shared to a production team hungry for drama, and pray she doesn't hate me more when the cameras stop rolling. Also in that time, I have to convince myself I can keep my hands off her long enough to say the words I should have said a decade ago.

By the end of this, I either finally get her back, or I could lose her forever. I'm willing to do whatever it takes for the former, even if it means making an ass of myself to do it.

I close my eyes, the ghost of her scent—vanilla and jasmine—curling through my memory like smoke.

"Send me the contract," I say.

Alex lets out a shaky laugh. "You're serious?"

"Dead serious."

Another exhale, this one almost relieved. "Okay. I'll email it tonight. Nondisclosure is ironclad. You breathe a word of this before the reveal, we're both done."

"Understood."

"And, Scott?" His voice drops, quieter now. "I'm glad you're doing this."

I end the call before he can say anything else.

The phone clatters onto the desk. My heart is still hammering, a violent rhythm that echoes in every inch of my skin. I stare at the dark screen, seeing nothing but her—Lyla Clark, ten years older, ten years more beautiful, ten years more dangerous to me than she ever was at eighteen.

I'm going to see her again. Going to touch her again. And this time, I'm not walking away.

Chapter Two

Off the coast of Belize
Two weeks later
Day One

Lyla

The speedboat cuts through water so clear it looks fake.

Sunlight fractures over the surface, throwing silver onto my knees and the white deck beneath my sandals. The island ahead is exactly what the casting ad promised—white beach, emerald jungle, a villa perched high on the cliffs like it's watching us arrive.

Paradise.

I grip the railing anyway.

Two weeks ago, my biggest crisis involved a bride sobbing over ivory versus cream napkins. Now I'm headed toward a reality dating show I applied to at three in the morning because desperation makes people brave—or stupid.

"Ten days in paradise to find love?" Emily laughs beside me, her raven hair snapping in the wind. "This feels too good to be true."

If it's too good to be true, it usually is.

I smooth my sundress over my thighs and inhale slowly, grounding myself. I didn't come here for romance. I came here for leverage.

One hundred thousand dollars and national exposure could take my business to new heights. It could buy me staff, breathing room, a future that doesn't require me to keep sprinting on fumes.

For once, I want something that's just...good.

The dock comes into view.

Cameras line it.

Not a couple of handhelds for behind-the-scenes footage. Real rigs. Boom mics. The kind of setup that makes your skin tighten because it's not casual.

This is definitely not low-budget.

A production assistant beams as she helps us off the boat. "Welcome to Paradise Found! You're our first arrivals!"

The other contestants file onto the terrace with me—Sean, Bradley, Zayne, Jessa, and Emily—faces bright with that specific blend of nervous excitement and hunger people wear when they know they're being watched.

I tell myself my smile is normal. Tell myself my heart isn't racing.

The host appears like she's been conjured: Miranda. Glossy hair, glossy lips, glossy confidence. She moves like she's hosting an awards show, not orchestrating emotional chaos.

"I can already feel the chemistry," she purrs.

I clock the way her gaze lingers—not flirtatious. Measuring. Cataloging. The same look I've seen from vendors who smile while quietly inflating invoices.

Cocktails appear. The afternoon unfolds with a strange ease.

Sean talks about travel. Zayne does impressions. Bradley shocks everyone by knowing every word to a Broadway show.

For the first time in months, no one needs me to fix anything.

I'm just Lyla.

And for a few minutes, I can almost forget why I'm here.

Miranda claps her hands. "Contestants, our next arrival is here!"

We migrate toward the terrace railing, drinks in hand. Someone makes a joke about "first impressions." Someone else laughs too loudly.

The stairs below the terrace come into view. A man climbs them, polished and confident, smile already in place—until his gaze lands on Emily.

The smile fractures.

"Emily," he breathes, like her name is a bruise.

Emily's drink slips from her fingers. Glass shatters against the stone.

"Trevor?" Her voice comes out thin. "What are you—What are you doing here?"

Trevor's composure wobbles. "You applied, too?"

Around us, the air shifts. The laughter dies. The cameras seem louder.

"You two know each other?" Bradley asks carefully.

"We dated," Emily replies flatly.

Trevor looks like he wants to explain. Emily looks like she wants to burn the terrace down.

One ex-couple. That's odd. Is this some kind of twist they're introducing to make the show more entertaining?

Miranda's smile doesn't change.

"Contestants, our next arrival is here!"

Another figure comes up the stairs—tall, composed, the kind of woman who knows exactly how she looks on camera and uses it. She freezes when she reaches the terrace, eyes locking on Bradley.

Her expression flashes shock.

Then she smooths it into something sharp and controlled.

"Well," she says lightly, "this is unexpected."

Bradley goes rigid beside me. "What the fuck are you doing here, Renee?"

Renee arches a brow. "Seems we're both looking for love in paradise."

The silence that follows is loaded. A history you can't see but can feel.

Two. Coincidence is starting to lose credibility.

Miranda claps again. "Next arrival!"

A third person appears.

Sean's easy grin vanishes so fast it's like someone cut it off. His shoulders lock.

"No," he mutters under his breath.

The woman steps onto the terrace and lifts her head.

"Sean."

His throat works. "Valerie."

Valerie's gaze flicks briefly to the cameras, then back to him. "So this is why you ghosted me."

Sean's face goes pale. "I-I didn't know you'd be here."

"Funny," Valerie's smile is cool, practiced. "I thought the same thing."

Three.

My stomach tightens. A hollow weight settles under my ribs.

This isn't random.

Miranda's expression is too pleased. Too expectant. Like she's watching dominoes fall exactly the way she set them up.

"Our next arrival is here!"

A man climbs the stairs—handsome in a safe, guy-next-door way. He reaches the terrace smiling like he's ready to be introduced.

Then he sees Jessa, and the smile collapses.

Jessa inhales sharply beside me. Her fingers curl into her palm like she's holding herself in place.

"Nick," she says, and her voice is pure disdain.

He stops. His gaze sharpens. "You're here. How have you been?" he asks, like this is normal.

Jessa lets out a humorless laugh. "Fine. Not that you ever gave a shit."

Four.

The sunlight feels too bright now. The ocean too loud. The terrace too small.

By the time Miranda announces the next arrival, no one reacts. We're all braced.

A woman comes up the stairs fast, heels snapping against stone, anger practically radiating off her. She doesn't scan the terrace—She zeroes in.

Her eyes lock on Zayne. A smile curls on her lips like a weapon.

Zayne stiffens. "You've got to be shitting me."

She squeals like she's delighted. "Zany bear! I've missed you so much!"

"Kylie," he says, voice dragging with dread.

Five.

I don't have to count anymore to know what that means.

Six women, including me. Five exes have already appeared.

There's one left.

My breath goes shallow. I take a sip of my drink, and it tastes like nothing. My pulse thuds at the base of my throat.

I don't look at Miranda. I don't need her confirmation to know the next person up those stairs is mine.

The only question is which ghost they dug up.

I tell myself it won't be Scott. It can't be. I've spent ten years building a life where he doesn't exist. Spent that time making sure he couldn't undo me with a look. I've spent—

A man appears at the base of the stairs.

Broad shoulders under a dress shirt. Sleeves rolled to the forearms. The kind of build that isn't just from a gym—discipline, repetition, something earned the hard way.

His stride is long and deliberate, every step purposeful.

He doesn't look at the cameras, much less scan the group like the others did. His attention is already narrowed, locked somewhere ahead.

My stomach drops.

Please don't let it be—

He comes closer. Details sharpen. Dark hair cut short. A jaw that looks harder than I remember. A body built thick through the chest and arms like time carved him into something more dangerous.

He reaches the top step and lifts his head.

His eyes find mine.

Blue. Striking. Familiar in the worst way. It hits like a wave.

Scott Bennett steps onto the terrace.

Ten years collapse into nothing like time has never passed.

Sound drains away. The ocean blurs. The villa tilts slightly, like my body can't decide whether to run or freeze.

He looks older. Taller. Broader. The softness that used to live around his mouth is gone, replaced by something sharpened and controlled.

His gaze holds mine. And then his mouth curves—slow, deliberate. Unapologetic. Not hesitant. As though he's been waiting for this moment.

"Hello, everyone," he says calmly. "I'm Scott."

He doesn't look at anyone but me when he says it.

My champagne flute slips from my fingers. Crystal explodes against stone.

Someone says my name. It could be Emily. It could be the host. It could be a producer sprinting toward me.

I can't hear any of it.

All I can hear is my pulse roaring in my ears.

Scott's eyes dip briefly to the shattered glass, then lift back to my face as if he's taking me in. As if he's allowed.

My skin goes tight.

Heat unfurls low in my body—slow, unmistakable, treacherous. It slides downward, curling between my thighs like my body is betraying me before my brain can catch up.

No. Absolutely not.

I clamp my thighs together and force my shoulders back. Force my face into something controlled.

"You," I manage, and my voice comes out thin.

He steps closer. Not rushing. Not crowding.

But his presence fills the space like it always did—solid, overwhelming, and inevitable.

"Lyla," he says quietly.

My name on his lips sounds different now. Lower. Rougher. Like it's been carried around in his throat for a decade.

My breath catches.

Dampness gathers between my legs in a humiliating rush. My nipples tighten beneath the thin fabric of my dress.

My body remembers.

My body is a dumbass.

"What are you doing here?" My voice is sharper now. Better.

He doesn't answer right away.

He takes another step. Close enough that I catch his scent—cedar, spice, something clean and male underneath. A memory slams into me: his truck, summer nights, his hands on my hips.

Anger flares, hot and saving.

"I asked you a question," I snap. "Don't avoid it."

His jaw tightens, but he doesn't look away.

"I came for you."

The words hit hard. My mind scrambles for logic.

He didn't come for me when I cried myself to sleep. He didn't come for me when I begged the universe for an explanation. He didn't come for me for ten years. And now he's standing here in front of cameras like he's allowed to make a claim.

My anger surges.

"You knew?" I hiss, and I hate that my voice shakes. "You knew this was what the show really was, and you still came?"

His eyes narrow slightly. "Yes."

Betrayal slices clean through me, sharper than the abandonment ever was because it's present. Tangible. In my face.

"You don't ambush someone on cable television just to have a conversation," I bite out.

"I'm not asking to start over without explaining," he says, controlled. "You deserve to know what happened."

"Why does that matter now?"

His throat works. For the first time, something flickers in his expression—pain, maybe. Or frustration.

"Please," he says, and the word is quiet enough it feels private. "Give me time to explain."

Time.

The very thing he stole.

I shake my head. "You ran out of time the moment you left."

His gaze holds mine like he's trying to reach through me. "There are things you don't know."

"Stop," I snap. "Don't pretend you get to decide what I deserve. You don't know me anymore."

Before he can respond, Miranda clears her throat, slicing through the moment like a blade.

I tear my gaze from Scott and turn on her.

She's smiling. Like this is delightful.

"What a perfect way to end our arrivals!" she trills. "And just think —this is only the beginning."

I want to throttle her.

Not just for me. For Emily's shattered glass. For Renee's tight smile. For Sean's haunted face. For the way the air feels like a trap.

Miranda corrals all twelve of us into a loose circle. Cameras shift. Boom mics dip closer.

"Now that we're all here," she begins, "I have something to confess."

No shit.

"When you applied for *Paradise Found*, we told you that you were signing up for a tropical singles dating show." She pauses like she's savoring her confession. "Well...we weren't entirely honest."

Around me, voices rise—cursing, protesting, demanding contracts and lawyers.

Miranda lifts a hand, still smiling. "*Paradise Found* never existed. It was a cover."

My stomach drops lower.

"Welcome," she says brightly, "to *The One That Got Away*—the show that reunites you with your most significant lost love."

The terrace erupts.

Trevor starts swearing. Renee looks like she might punch someone. Sean goes stiff. Kylie laughs like it's a gift from the universe.

And Scott—He doesn't move. His gaze stays on me like the rest of the world is background noise.

My anger turns cold.

"This is insane," I say, stepping forward. "I'm leaving. Now."

It's not a negotiation as I choose to act on instinct.

Scott lifts his hand like he's going to stop me. Then he catches himself and drops it to his side.

"Lyla—"

"Don't," I warn, not looking at him. "Don't say my name."

I scan for the nearest producer, the nearest exit, any sign of control.

Miranda appears at my side like she's been waiting. "I'm afraid leaving isn't an option, sweetie."

I turn on her, fury sharp. "I hate to break it to you, *sweetie*, but I can and I will. Watch me."

I start to move past her.

"Leave now," she says, voice still syrupy, "and you'll have to pay the penalty clause in your contract."

I roll my eyes. "Send me a bill."

"All two hundred fifty thousand or in increments?"

I stop cold.

The number doesn't compute at first. It's too ridiculous—until it does sink in.

My throat goes dry.

"What did you just say?"

"Your contract includes a penalty clause for an unexpected but voluntary departure." Miranda repeats, like she's explaining a return policy.

"For two hundred fifty thousand?" My laugh is sharp and humorless. "That's more than the prize."

"It's our policy."

My stomach turns.

I can't afford that. Not in my worst nightmare.

Around me, the other contestants are doing the same math. The same panic. Trapped by signatures and fine print and desperation.

Miranda claps her hands again, bright as ever. "Now, let's establish our villa couples."

Of course. Once they trap you with money, they trap you even more with proximity.

"Each woman will draw a number," she explains, holding up a velvet pouch. "Number one gets first choice of any man. Number two can choose from the remaining...or steal number one's choice."

Strategic warfare disguised as romance.

A few minutes later, my hands feel cold as I step forward with the other women, drawing slips in order.

Renee draws first. Valerie second. Emily third. Jessa Fourth.

My fingers dip into the pouch.

Paper slides against my skin.

I unfold my slip.

I'm fifth.

Kylie is last to draw, making her last to choose.

My pulse doesn't slow. It spikes.

I scan the line of men with a sinking feeling as choices happen fast. Steals happen faster. Partners shift like pieces on a board.

When it's my turn, my options are already narrowing. Unless I choose to steal, it's down to Scott and Zayne—and I'd rather not lose an arm by these fierce women.

Scott stands there like he already knows. His mouth has that faint curve again. Certainty. As though he's been waiting for me to be forced into his orbit.

Not a chance in hell.

"Zayne," I say quickly, choosing literally anyone else.

Zayne steps toward me with visible relief.

Kylie is last to choose, and she doesn't even pretend to consider. "I'm stealing Zayne."

Zayne's shoulders slump. "I'm so sorry," he mutters as he steps away.

And suddenly I'm standing alone.

Miranda's smile widens like she just won. "That leaves our final couple," she announces. "Lyla and Scott."

The cameras zoom. Someone whistles. Someone else laughs nervously.

Scott steps toward me. His gaze drops briefly to my mouth, then lifts back to my eyes.

"Hello, little one," he murmurs.

Heat flickers low in my belly, immediate and unwanted.

Hearing his pet name for me, something I haven't heard since he left, hits me hard. I let out a small gasp.

I quickly harden my expression and glare up at him. "Don't call me that."

His voice drops, rougher. "We're going to have plenty of time to talk now."

"The hell we are," I say through my teeth.

He doesn't argue. He just watches me like he's already memorized every escape route I might take.

~

Scott

One king bed. One couch.

That's the first thing I register when the bedroom door shuts behind us.

The room is too intimate for strangers and too small for history like ours. White walls. Open beams. Gauzy curtains lifting in the ocean breeze. The bed sits centered beneath a slow-turning fan, an soft ivory comforter over crisp sheets as though deliberately designed to encourage something to happen.

It won't. Not like that.

Lyla steps inside without looking at me. Chin high. Spine straight. Every inch of her posture says she's bracing for negotiation, not proximity.

The cameras in the corners blink red.

I clock every angle automatically. Lens height. Microphone placement. Window sightlines. Blind spots. Old habits. Old training. My body doesn't know how not to assess threat.

She moves toward the dresser and sets her bag down with controlled precision. Not a single wasted motion. The same woman who can rebuild a torn wedding gown under pressure and make it look effortless.

"Say it," she says, still facing away from me.

Her voice is level. That's how I know she's furious.

"Say what?"

"That you planned this." She turns slowly. Her eyes are sharp, wounded beneath them. "That you knew and decided ambushing me on television was the best way to start a conversation."

I shut the door fully and lean back against it, giving her space. Giving her the illusion of control.

"I knew," I say. There's no point in softening that. "But it's not like I planned the room assignment."

A humorless laugh escapes her. "That's supposed to make it better?"

"No." I hold her gaze. "It's supposed to be honest."

Her mouth parts like she didn't expect the answer. I shouldn't notice. I do anyway.

God, she's beautiful.

Not the way she was at eighteen. Not soft and bright-eyed, looking at me like I hung the damn moon. This version of her is sharpened. Controlled. Her hair falls over one shoulder in deliberate waves. Her sundress skims her waist and clings to curves that didn't exist back then. Blood immediately rushes south at the sight.

Focus.

"You don't decide what I deserve or get to dictate when I'm ready to hear anything."

"I know."

"Do you?" She steps closer. Not enough to touch. Enough to test. "Because it feels like you decided that for me again."

That lands.

The room feels smaller.

"I'm not here to force anything," I say carefully. "I'm here because silence didn't fix it."

Her eyes narrow at me. "Silence didn't fix it because you were the silence."

I inhale slowly through my nose. I could push. But I see it in her face —She's not ready for explanations. Not here. Not like this.

"You're right," I say. "I left. I didn't explain. I own that."

Her eyes flicker. Surprise. As though she was ready for an argument.

"Then I think you should leave." she presses.

"I can't."

"Why not?"

Because I can't breathe in a world where you think I didn't choose you.

Because I've replayed the look on your face for ten years.

Because I would burn down anything that threatens you.

"You heard what Miranda said. That penalty clause is insane," I point out. Technically, it's not a lie. And this still gives me a legitimate reason to be "stuck" here.

"You've already disappeared once, I'm sure you can figure it out."

I let out a deep sigh. "You know it's not that simple."

She steps closer again, anger rising. "Oh, please. How complicated can ghosting someone be? You're already good at it."

There's more to what happened then, more than she knows.

I glance at the camera in the corner. The red light steady. Listening. Recording. This is the first real conversation we've had in a decade, and I'd rather it not happen under surveillance, much less for the world's entertainment.

Her laugh is brittle. "Of course it's *not that simple*. Convenient."

"It's not about convenience. I just can't spend six-figures willy-nilly." I could, but that's beside the point.

I push off the door slowly, hands visible. Intentional.

She studies me for a long beat, as though searching for some angle I might have.

Her lips press together in a tight line.

"I guess that makes sense," she yields, staring between the couch and the bed.

"I'm sleeping on the couch," I state before she can argue.

Her brows lift slightly. "You don't have to."

"I want to."

That's the truth. Her comfort will always come before my own.

Also, the bed is too close. Too dangerous. I don't trust myself not to move toward her in the middle of the night like muscle memory never died. I don't trust myself not to slide my hand over her skin and convince her with touch instead of words.

She studies me.

The ocean outside crashes softly. The fan hums overhead. I can hear her breathing. Shallow. Controlled.

"I'm going to shower," she says finally, like it's a power move.

"Okay." I nod.

She hesitates, as though waiting for resistance.

She won't get any from me.

Grabbing her toiletry bag, she disappears into the bathroom and shuts the door behind her. A second later, water turns on.

I exhale.

The room smells faintly like salt and something floral from her skin. I drag a hand down my face and push off toward the couch.

It's small. Narrow. The kind of furniture meant for decoration, not sleep.

Good. Discomfort is an old friend anyway.

The shower runs steadily behind the wall. I try not to let myself picture her under it, but my mind wanders anyway.

Water sliding over her shoulders. Down the curve of her back. Over the swell of her hips. Her head tipped back. Lips parted. Skin flushed from heat.

Fuck me.

My cock turns hard as stone, pressing against the zipper of my jeans.

I grip the back of the couch until my knuckles go white.

Ten fucking years and I still crave her like this.

A few minutes later, the shower shuts off.

My pulse kicks up.

A few seconds later, the bathroom door opens.

Silk.

That's what hits me first.

She's wearing pale silk pajamas. A loose tank with thin straps. Shorts that barely cover the tops of her thighs. The fabric catches the light, skimming her skin in a way that feels deliberately unfair.

My gaze drops before I can stop it.

Her legs are bare. Smooth. Familiar.

The silk clings slightly at her hips. The curve of her waist. The faint outline of her breasts beneath the too-loose fabric.

My throat goes dry.

"Stop looking at me like that," she says, but her voice isn't steady. Could she be just as affected by me as I am by her?

"Like what?" My voice comes out lower than I intend.

"Like I'm—" She cuts herself off.

Like you're mine.

Old instinct surges hard and possessive in my chest. I have to force myself to stare back at her face.

"Old habits," I say quietly.

Her breath catches.

She turns away from me too quickly and crosses to the bed, pulling back the covers and slipping in. The mattress dips. Sheets rustle.

She turns onto her side with her back facing me. She establishes distance.

Grabbing a pillow and blanket from the closet, I set up on the couch. It creaks under my weight.

She stiffens at the sound.

"You don't have to martyr yourself," she mutters.

"It's not martyrdom."

"Then what is it?"

Restraint.

Because if I climb in that bed, I'll want to fulfill all the unspeakable things I want to do to you.

"I'm not going to make you more uncomfortable than you already are," I say.

Silence settles again.

The space between us feels charged. Not empty. Alive. Every shift of fabric, every breath, every small sound amplified.

Minutes pass.

I know she's awake. I can feel it. The tension hums through the room like an exposed wire.

"Scott?"

"Yes, little one?"

"You said you came onto this show for me? What do you mean by that?"

"I've always cared about you," I say evenly.

She goes still.

"That's not what I asked."

"I know."

"Then answer me."

I grit my teeth. The urge to explain claws up my throat. I bury it.

"I can't. Not like this."

Her voice hardens. "You mean not on your timeline."

"No." I turn my head slightly, just enough to look at her silhouette in the dark. "Not in a room that profits off it."

Silence.

"Then when?" she presses. "When it's easier for you? When there aren't cameras everywhere? If you're looking for a way for the producers not to find out, you'll be waiting for ten days."

I hold her gaze in the dark.

"I'm not waiting," I say quietly. "I'm not running out a clock. And I'm not looking for a loophole." My voice stays even. Controlled. "I'll tell you. Soon. I'll find a way."

"How soon?" she demands.

"When I can also look at you and know you're hearing me—not reacting to my words."

"And if I don't care about that?" she challenges.

"You will."

Her breathing stutters.

The words land heavy between us.

The space between us feels charged, alive with everything unsaid.

I could cross it, but I don't.

"If I wait," I add quietly, "it won't be forever."

Silence stretches.

"So not tonight?" she whispers.

"No," I agree, voice rougher now. "Not tonight."

The fan keeps turning.

The ocean keeps crashing.

And the distance between us stays exactly where she needs it—even if it costs me everything to hold it there.

Chapter Three

Day Two

Lyla

The morning sun is merciless against my eyes as I walk down to the villa's kitchen for breakfast. The place hums with two spectrums of controlled chaos: the contestants fill their breakfast plates, nursing hangovers, while the crew murmurs to each other and coordinates which camera goes where.

I sit at the foot of the table, absentmindedly eating a plate of eggs that have long gone cold.

If I have a couple of those citrus margaritas I saw sitting on the bar, would it make this situation any better? Probably not, though the thought is tempting.

Being on a reality dating show is crazy. But being on a dating show with your ex is insane and filled with nothing but headaches. Why didn't I see it coming? Why didn't I smell the bullshit when it was practically staring me in the face?

There was no way I could have known.

That may be true, but it doesn't change the fact that I slept in the same room with Scott Bennett for the first time in a decade.

I barely slept, if I did at all. And even when I did drift off, Scott's even breathing and soft snoring were right there to wake me back up again. But it wasn't the volume that kept me up. It was the fact that he was even in the room in the first place.

The low creak of the couch when he shifted... His proximity is now so close, it freaks me out. Close enough to reach—and far enough to remind me why I built my walls in the first place.

I hear strong, deliberate footsteps behind me, coming closer. Then before I can blink, I see a muscular hand take the plate in front of me, replacing it with a strawberry yogurt with granola on top.

My favorite. Where did he get that?

I searched high and low for some, but the kitchen swore up and down they didn't have any.

I don't turn around.

"If you're hoping to catch me off guard, you lost the element of surprise a while ago."

As if finding my favorite breakfast is going to get us back together.

His voice is against my ear, making me jump a little in surprise.

"Eat this. You're going to need your strength today."

Annoyed, I turn to face him.

Big mistake.

Seeing him at night for the first time in ten years is one thing. Seeing him in daylight for the first time in ten years makes what I feel so much worse. A white tank hugs his body, which looks like it's been carved by gods. His tanned skin glows in the sun's rays. I see more detail to his face. It's harder. Less boy. Those blue eyes lock onto mine, as though he could still stare into my soul. He seems more like a man who knows what he's capable of.

"Not hungry." My stomach growls as soon as the words leave my lips. I wince.

Why do I have to be my own traitor?

He hands me a spoon. His expression turns fixed, staring directly into my eyes. His voice goes down an octave. "Eat."

His response isn't a question. Not a mild suggestion. There's a powerfulness to his presence, his demand of me. It sends shivers up my spine, yet hurt curls low in my belly.

I just reunited with this man twelve hours ago, and he's already confusing me.

My breath catches. And his stare becomes more insistent the longer I don't eat.

Reluctantly, I scoop the yogurt onto the spoon, placing a large helping into my mouth. The yogurt melts onto my tongue, exactly the way I've always liked it. I can't help but moan as I take a second bite.

"Thank you," he sounds relieved as he takes the seat to my right, watching me eat. "And no, that's not what I was going for."

I swallow my second bite. "Then what are you going for? You have me trapped here. What's the next phase of your plan?"

"Lyla, despite what you may think, I don't have any ulterior motives against you."

"You ambushed me on cable television. That's one to start. So it only makes sense that you have another trick up your sleeve."

"I know me showing up was the last thing you expected, but I'm here to see you. There's so much I want to say. There's so much for you to know."

"And you thought telling me whatever bullshit story you think I want to hear on cable television was a great idea?"

He sighs. "I'll admit, the environment isn't ideal. But it couldn't wait."

I scoff. "Right, because ten years wasn't long enough of a wait for you."

"I'm here for you."

I shake my head at his words. "Given where we are, and how long you've been absent, forgive me if I don't believe you." I finish the last bite of my yogurt before resting the spoon against the rim of the bowl and setting it aside. "Even if you were telling me the truth, you only came for you. Let's face it; you left back then for greener pastures, and now that time has passed, you feel guilty for your adolescent impulses and came onto this show for closure or whatever version of redemption you think will help you sleep better at night."

His jaw tightens. "I know you have no reason to believe me, but I'm serious. And I don't need to be a TV personality for closure."

"Then what do you need? Because I certainly don't need you." I say the words, but deep down something in my gut tells me that's a lie. For a moment it irks me before I shove it down.

"You." He takes my hand. "I need you, Lyla."

The moment his hand makes contact with mine, the pool noise fades. My pulse stutters. I'm quick to pull it back.

"Don't."

"Don't what?"

"Don't say things like that. Things you don't mean."

"Why not?"

Because I might start to believe you.

Because I still remember exactly how your hands feel on me.

Because the bundle of nerves between my legs is craving for your touch.

I lift my chin. "Because you forfeited that right."

"Little one—"

"Don't call me that."

Silence falls between us. On the other side of the table, laughter and chatter erupt. A camera follows one of the guys with one of the girls. The world around us continues to move.

But here, between us, it's static.

"You can't just...show up and expect me to take you back like nothing happened."

He shakes his head. "I don't expect you to. But..." He lifts his hand, brushing two fingers lightly at my cheek, resting at my jaw. The contact is barely there yet electrifying all at once. "I have every intention of proving to you we belong together."

Heat floods over my skin. I can't move. I can't think of anything other than his touch, his stare, his words.

Is this man insane?

"You look flushed."

"You're imagining things," I deny.

His thumb presses lightly beneath my chin, forcing eye contact. His blue eyes are all I see.

The audacity of this man.

For a moment, I melt into his touch. Firm but gentle.

His gaze softens.

Heat curls and tightens low in my belly. My girl parts flutter.

Hell, no.

I'm only feeling this way because he's right there. My feelings for him died long ago. At least that's what I tell myself.

I quickly shove his hand away. "You're imagining things."

His stare turns incredulous. He makes it obvious I'm not that convincing.

"I could always read you. Still can."

I shake my head. Anger surges hot and saving. "I'm not the same girl you left behind."

"You're right; you're not. But I'd like to know the person you are now."

I scoff. "No thanks."

He had so long to get to know me then. To show his face. Instead, he chose now.

There was a time when I would have given him all of myself. But that was before. Before he left. Before silence carved me open. Before I bled alone.

I immediately stand from my seat, walking away from everyone. From him. Anywhere is better than under his exposing gaze.

He's way too close.

Seeing no physical person around, I walk over to the terrace and try to take deep breaths. I pace back and forth. My mind spirals in multiple directions.

I need to get off this island. But I'm stuck here—and I can't afford to spend six figures just to get away from a man.

Shit.

"Lyla."

I whirl to find him walking toward me. I groan.

"Just go away."

He shakes his head. "We both know that's not what you want."

"You don't know what I want. Not anymore."

He immediately closes the distance between us, and his eyes darken.

His stature towers over me possessively. His voice is low and rough. "I lost you once, little one. I'm going to win you back."

I cross my arms. Anything to get some distance. "And whose fault is that?"

His mouth flattens. "Entirely my own. I admit that."

Tense silence stretches between us. I hear muffled sounds of laughter erupting near the bar. Sounds of water splashing. The world keeps moving.

"You can't just pop back into my life and expect to pick up where we left off."

"That's not my intention. Too much has happened."

"Yes, it has." I stand my ground.

He lowers his gaze to my hand, taking it into his again.

I stiffen. I should pull back, but his grasp is warm, inviting.

When his gaze meets mine again, his lips are so close to mine. The heat of his body radiates over me. The pull I've been trying to ignore grows into an uncontrollable need.

My nipples tighten beneath the thin fabric of my swimsuit top. My breath goes shallow.

Damn him, damn my body.

"Time has changed us. Nothing may be the same," he says quietly. "But your body can't lie to me."

Without thinking, acting on impulse, I fist his shirt into my palms and shove him backward toward the nearest stone column. His back hits it with a dull thud.

I breathe heavily as I stare into this man.

For half a second, surprise flashes across his face. Then it's gone, replaced by something hot and dangerous.

"Tell me what you want, little one."

"You want to psychoanalyze me?"

His hands move to my waist, sliding down to my hips as he pulls me closer. Firm and removing every inch of space there is left between us.

"Tell me what you want," he repeats. His mouth brushes with mine until he claims it.

Out of instinct and familiarity, I press into him, into his kiss. My body arches.

His hands travel everywhere. One arm bands around my waist, hauling me impossibly close against him. The other fists in my hair, tugging gently at my scalp at a different angle.

His mouth opens against me, tasting of morning air and a musk that's distinctly him, male. This kiss is slow and intimate. He doesn't just claim; he explores. As if he's kissing me for the first time.

The world narrows to friction as his hand slides down and grips the back of my thigh, lifting and pressing it against him.

My body melts farther into him, remembering exactly how to. Like I've never left his body in the ten years we've been apart.

His mouth drags from my lips, down to my jaw, past my throat, and to the swells of my breasts.

I close my eyes to the feel of his mouth, his tongue, on my skin. So familiar yet different. Rather than fast, he's deliberately slow. Rather than erratic, he's meticulous. His pleasure in this moment is all I can focus on.

His teeth then graze lightly beneath my ear. I gasp.

I rock my hips forward, desperate for friction against his hard length under my bundle of nerves.

He stills me with his large hands on my hips as his lips crash back to mine. I whimper and moan.

For a moment, he pulls back. "Tell me to stop," he growls.

I can't. That's the problem.

My body hums, my skin electric. Every nerve ending is lit up like it's been asleep—and just woke up with ravenous thirst.

But this—this moment, this heat, this pleasure—doesn't fix anything. It can't answer why things happened the way they did, much less erase the silence I had to endure. And it sure as hell doesn't rebuild the trust that was lost.

I push against him, breaking from the kiss and his hold on my body. He doesn't resist or try to pull me back.

Cool air hits my damp lips. My pulse roars in my ears as I catch my breath. My thighs are trembling. I feel damp between my legs.

"This," I say, breath uneven, "is exactly the problem."

His chest rises and falls slowly, but his expression remains fixed. "What is? We both still want each other."

"That's not the point."

"I know it isn't. But I still want you. I always have." The admission hangs there for a beat.

"Wanting me physically doesn't get me to trust you."

"I more than want you like that. It's always been this way for me."

I scoff. "No, it hasn't. You just miss what you left behind. Hell, once you've had me in your bed, you'll get the hell out of Dodge and go on to the next girl."

"You think I'm that shallow? That I'm that fickle and careless with you?"

"I don't know. Because I don't know who you are anymore. And I haven't for a long time."

He goes silent, nodding. As though he's just realized something. "I'm never going to leave your side ever again."

"You already did once. Actions speaks louder than words."

His jaw tightens. "Things were very different then than they are now."

I shake my head. "I don't want to hear your excuses. Just admit that you left and now you're back for a good time. At this rate, telling me that ugly truth will sound more honest."

Behind us, a producer calls for contestants to gather for the first official challenge.

I don't hesitate to leave him there as I walk away and back toward the crowd of voices.

Moments later, I stand beside the female contestants as they stare apprehensively at the blindfolds in front of them—and the giant rope obstacle course. It stands tall and intimidating, stretching across a pool of water.

Scott steps in the circle beside me.

The trust I had with him was severed long ago. But with the way things are looking, I might have to trust him again.

Chapter Four

Scott

The challenge standing in front of me looks like something out of *American Ninja Warrior*. We're gathered at the far end of the villa where the cliffs drop sharply into the ocean. Ropes and narrow platforms are out at a point where it's more of a drop-off. Below, waves slap rocks in a steady rhythm that sounds deceptively calm from the height of one story at most.

Helmets and harnesses hang from metal hooks. Coiled ropes and planks are tied together to create bridges. And a line of black fabric blindfolds sits on silver trays in front of us like party favors. And not in a good way. My pulse ticks up as I map the course.

This is a two-person challenge without a doubt, given the blindfolds. The planks are wonky and separate on purpose. Lyla would be just nimble enough to get across. But given my own size, I'll probably struggle more, especially if I'm going to be blindfolded. At least that's how I think how this will go.

"Today's challenge tests trust, communication, and teamwork,"

Miranda announces. "In your assigned couples, one partner will be blindfolded while the other, on the ground level, will verbally navigate their partner across this suspended obstacle course, down the final descent, and into the water. Once the course begins, no physical contact is allowed. And if you or your partner falls"—she gestures lightly toward the deep water below—"you will be disqualified from the challenge."

A ripple of tension moves through the group.

Trevor raises his hand. "So the blindfolded partner has to rely completely on the other's verbal guidance?"

Miranda nods once. "At the halfway point, you'll switch roles. First team to finish wins an overnight getaway. All-inclusive luxury hotel, private beach, couples massage, and gourmet dinner."

I look over at Lyla beside me. Color drains from her face for a beat before she smooths her expression into something neutral. She hasn't looked at me once since that kiss.

The memory flashes hot and fast—her mouth open under mine, her fingers grip my shirt into fists, her soft curves press firmly against me, the sweet whimpers and moans that made my cock hard and ready to claim her.

A trust exercise. With Lyla. Clearly, the irony isn't lost on either of us.

Twenty-four hours alone with Lyla, without any interference from other contestants, would be all I need to not just explain what happened between us ten years ago, but also—maybe, just maybe—find some reconciliation. I don't expect to fix what's been broken overnight, to win her heart back, but with the right words, it could be a step in the right direction at rekindling what we had. And this time, I could give her everything that I couldn't then.

Lyla grabs the silky blindfold with one hand, looking up at me with apprehension. The thought of Lyla blindfolded, helpless, and having no choice but to follow my every command has me reeling with anticipation. My cock hardens painfully against my trunks.

"I'll go first," I offer, stepping forward and grabbing the blindfold.

I notice her at the corner of my eye watching me. She exhales as though sighing in relief. "Fine."

You're not off the hook yet, little one.

Before I put on the blindfold, I look to her. She inhales sharply under my gaze.

"I trust you." And then darkness envelops me.

Moments later, I hear a whistle indicating the challenge has begun. But the second we start, I nearly misstep.

"There are some planks ahead," Lyla yells to me. "So... yeah."

I stop. "Little one, I need more information than that."

"What? You want a play-by-play?"

"Tell me what's in front of me."

She huffs out a sigh like I've inconvenienced her. "Planks."

No shit.

"They're very...planky," she adds.

I turn in the direction of her voice. "Did you just describe wood as 'planky'?"

"I'm a wedding planner, not a carpenter. Not that you'd know."

If only she knew...

I can't help but smirk. "Keep talking. I need your voice."

She scoffs. "That's funny, because you didn't seem to need it for a decade."

Despite her lack of guidance, I try to move anyway. With the dragging of my feet across the planks and my hands holding the rope on either side of me, I'm able to move at least five steps from where I started. But each step costs me my balance.

I wobble before finding my footing again. I bite back a curse.

"Oh." She feigns innocence with sarcasm in her voice. "Was I supposed to help?"

That bratty attitude would sound very different over my knee.

But as much as I'd love to imagine that or make it reality, the chances of that happening are slim to none. At least for now.

I manage to steady myself again before I come across what feels like a gap of open air under my foot.

"Lyla, what's happening?"

I'm met with silence for a long moment before I hear an extensive sigh.

"There's a gap under your foot. Stretch out your leg. A little more. Yes. Right there."

Following her instructions, I feel my foot eventually meet solid wood.

"Okay, couples!" Miranda's peppy voice reaches my ears. "Time to switch!"

Finally.

I pull off the blindfold and turn to Lyla as she walks through the obstacle course to me. Anticipation coils tight in my chest.

She looks like she'd rather face the obstacle course alone than hand control over to me.

Moments later, I secure the helmet on her head, while someone from the crew releases me from the harness, and straps her in. Despite the producer's insistence the obstacle course is safe, I test the knots around her—nice and tight. But that doesn't stop the growing need to get her off of the potential death trap.

When I'm satisfied, I hand her the blindfold. "Your turn, little one."

"Let's just get this over with." She tries to swipe it from my hand.

I pull away. "Let me put it on for you."

She tries to take it from my hands again. "No. I can do it on my own."

Is that how you've been going through life since I've been gone?

Her tone is dismissive, but she doesn't look away. Doesn't retreat. She just stands there, watching me like she's testing how much I'll push.

I give in, handing her the blindfold. "Suit yourself."

Switching positions, I come down to ground level as she settles into position.

I watch intently as she raises the blindfold to her face and over her eyes. It changes her expression instantly. When her eyes are covered, the sharpness in her expression disappears. Her breathing shifts subtly. Her lips part slightly.

She looks so vulnerable. Hell, yes!

"As a reminder to everyone, no touching your partner once the challenge continues," Miranda states. "And if one or both of you falls, you both will be out of the running to win this challenge."

Feeling satisfied that the harness has her secured, I step back and off the set of stairs.

When the whistle sounds again, Lyla grips the ropes on either side of her, seemingly frozen in fear. "I-I can't do this."

"Yes, you can, just relax and follow my voice."

"Relax? Yeah right."

"There are three wooden planks ahead of you," I explain with careful detail. "Each are about a few inches apart. They're stable. Take a step for me."

She swallows, remains frozen in place.

"Lyla, just walk straight steps for me. I'm not going to let you fall, little one."

"How can I trust that?"

"Think about it. Why would I let you fall?"

She sighs and hangs her head. Then, as if she's contemplating on what to do, she takes a step. The tip of her left foot taps on the first plank, like she's trying to feel where it is, before she settles her entire foot on it. Then she repeats that with her right foot on the next plank.

Maybe my adrenaline is spiking, or maybe I don't like her up there, but the ocean seems louder now, wind pushing salt air up the cliff face. Her hand shakes toward where the rope railing should be but stops short.

"Oh, my god. Oh, god." She begins to panic.

Without thinking, I rush toward her. But I'm stopped at the sound of Miranda reminding me of the rule.

Fuck.

I glare at her, then look back to Lyla.

"Something's wrong," Lyla panics again. "I can't feel anything under my foot." She hovers the tip of her sneaker over a gap in the rope.

"Move your foot two inches to your left," I instruct.

Nodding, she eventually finds the plank, sighing in relief.

"Good girl. Now, keep your shoulders square."

"Okay, I think I got this," Lyla hollers to me.

Uhh...what?

The girl still has a ways to go—blindfolded—and she thinks she can cross this course on her own?

"Love the confidence, doll, but I disagree."

She scoffs. "Of course you would."

When she makes it to the next step, she begins to wobble. She gasps. Her whole body shakes as the plank shifts slightly.

My pulse spikes. "Lyla, stop. You're going to fall."

She ignores me and keeps going.

"Lyla, I need you to stop," I repeat, dropping my voice down an octave. "You're going to fall, and we're going to lose."

She stops and pauses "We're going to lose? All the more reason."

It's like...she wants to lose.

Is that her plan? Is that what this defiance is about?

"Despite what you may think, I can do this my—"

Before she can finish that sentence, she reaches out a foot, and it only hits air. She puts her pointed foot out in multiple directions only to come to the same conclusion. What she doesn't realize, and only I can see, is that she has to balance on a rope at the far left.

I sigh. Clearly my point has been made. "Adjust your right foot half an inch forward and just slightly to your left. There's a knot in the wood."

She remains frozen in place, fear etched across her face despite the blindfold. Silence stretches between us except for wind and water below.

"As much as you don't care about winning, you and I both know you don't want to fall. So with that said...you're going to have to trust me."

Her laugh is brittle. "That's rich."

Beside me, I can hear Sean murmuring something to a producer. Valerie's voice floats faintly. The world narrows until it's just Lyla on these planks—and the drop directly beneath her. Where one misstep could easily have her toppling over and into the ocean. We're not high enough up for anyone to get hurt but just enough to make me nervous.

Despite my insistence, she steps again.

The course shifts from planks to suspended rope circles. They sway more visibly and will no doubt be harder for her to find her footing.

"Lyla, I know I'm the last voice you want to hear telling you what to do, but for the sake of your safety, listen to me. You're about to come across a rope ring."

"Sure. Thanks for the tip." She dismisses my warning.

Just as she's on the last plank, I yell, "Step down six inches and stretch out your foot. Find the center of the circle before you put your weight on it."

"I told you, I don't need—" When she casually reaches her foot out, she must realize a plank is no longer in front of her because her breathing changes. She clenches the rope around her.

The rope fibers brush her calf as she lowers her foot. The ring swings, taking her body with it. Her breath shakes; she lets out a gasp of fear.

Something in my chest twists. "Easy, baby. It'll move. That's normal. Just bend your knees, and it'll right itself. Don't make any sudden movements."

The ring tilts. She grabs at air instinctively.

"You're clear," I say immediately. "You're centered. Don't lock your legs."

"You sound awfully sure of yourself," she says skeptically.

"I am."

"And why is that?"

"Because if you fall, I'm going in after you."

She remains silent, her mouth in a tight line, as she rights herself and reaches her other foot, which was still on the plank, out for the next ring. Her knuckles are white as a ghost as she grasps the top rope around her.

When her open foot finally does meet the next ring, it sways harder. Wind kicks up off the water. A spray of salt water hits her bare legs. But she maintains her balance.

I've almost breathed a sigh of relief when she misjudges the distance, and her foot lands half on the top edge, making the ring jerk violently from underneath her.

Her body pitches forward, making her scream in fear. Arms flail.

My pulse detonates.

"Lyla!" For half a second, I'm ready to fuck the rules when she manages to steady herself again—barely. Her breathing is ragged, her body shaking.

This is torture more for me than it is for her.

"I-I can't see. Oh, god," she yells in terror.

"I know, baby girl. But please listen to me. You're going to hurt yourself."

Silence falls between us. The producers whisper behind me. I can feel cameras angling for the moment.

"This is bullshit," she says under her breath.

"Just keep going. You're almost at the end."

Her head tilts slightly toward my voice. "How do I know you're not screwing me over?"

What is she talking about? "If I was, why would I be trying to help you cross?"

"Why should I trust you?"

"Sweetheart, you think I'm an oblivious idiot?" I pinch the bridge of my nose. "Arguing with me will only keep you where you are. If you want off, you're going to have to trust me to get you across."

Perhaps seeing my point, she takes in a deep frustrated sigh. "Fine. Tell me what I need to do."

Thank you.

"Move up slightly forward and then to the left. Your left foot should touch another ring. Make sure your foot is centered on the ring before you put your weight on it."

She nods but slightly hesitates. "Tell me when my foot is hovering over it."

"I will."

Moving slowly forward, she does what I ask as I verbally guide her to where her foot is centered on the rope ring.

I give her my next set of instructions. "In your next three steps, you'll come to a beam. It's wide enough to plant your foot on it."

"O-okay," she replies.

She makes quick work toward the beam, gaining momentum. I let myself breathe a sigh of relief when the beam tilts under her weight.

Shit.

Lyla tries to balance herself but overcorrects.

"Scott—" She loses her grip. That harness jerks tight against the rope as she slips sideways. Her body swings over open space. The top catches her mid-drop. The sound of it snapping taut echoes against the small cliff.

She screams.

My heart stops.

She dangles for a split second above the open water, lavender hair whipping in the wind, breath punched from her lungs.

"Pull her!" a producer shouts.

I'm already moving.

They lower her fast as she hits the water, the ripples consuming her whole.

I don't think. I dive. Cold water slams into my chest. Salt burns my eyes.

I'm quick to surface with my arm around her waist while I swim us to safety. Her body is pressed up against mine as she rips the blindfold off.

Her eyes are wide as she coughs. She shakes as I hold her close against my chest. Her chest heaves rapidly against my chest. A stunned, almost blank stare forms on her face as though processing what just happened.

"I got you. I got you," I softly assure repeatedly as the crew guides me to a dock. Cameras hover.

For a moment, her gaze locks onto my face. The tightness in her brows softens as she looks at me with something like disbelief. As though she is searching for answers. Then she breaks the spell, pushing herself out of my arms.

"Let go of me," she demands, her chin lifted slightly. "I can swim on my own just fine."

"Good for you, but I'm not letting go. You might have hurt yourself."

When we reach the dock, I guide her to the connecting metal ladder. After climbing up, she quickly takes a few steps away from me, adjusting her soaked hair that clings to her neck. As though pretending nothing happened.

We make it back to the beginning of the course when Miranda yells, "Time! Jessa and Nick are the winners!"

Cheers erupt.

Lyla doesn't react. Instead, she looks at me with fury blazing in her eyes.

Why is she mad at me? She wanted this to happen. Then again, what if that's not the reason? Could she be mad because I saved her? Yet that doesn't make any sense either. Could she be mad...at herself?

"The rest of the day is yours, contestants, to relax and mingle. Head back to the villa," Miranda instructs.

Before I have a chance to think further, is the first to start the trek back to the villa without another word. An angry scowl forms on her face.

As I follow closely behind, a thought comes to mind. No matter what I do, no matter how many challenges there are where I can try to prove she can rely on me, Lyla doesn't trust me.

Not even close.

Chapter Five

Scott

I can smell Lyla's scent in the air as she walks past me and to the bar. Vanilla and jasmine fill my nostrils—the same scent that once clung to my clothes after she'd spent the night with me in my truck, under the stars. Despite the time away, the need to have her is still instant and demanding.

Watching Lyla from a distance the past twelve hours has become a given. She's not the only reason I'm here. But she's also the most, and only, tempting thing for me here.

But despite this, the pool deck is a battlefield disguised as relaxation.

Sunlight ricochets off the water hard enough to make my eyes narrow. Chlorine hangs sharp in the air, mixing with sunscreen and the salt carried up from the ocean below. Bodies are everywhere—loungers packed tight, bare skin gleaming with baby oil.

I sit back in a low teak chair, forearms braced on the arms, and watch.

Lyla is across the deck with Emily and Valerie, perched on the edge of the infinity pool, deep in conversation. Her legs are in the water, toes flexing lazily beneath the surface. Her lavender hair is damp at the ends, clinging to her collarbone.

Sunlight slides down the curve of her throat and disappears between her breasts before catching in the hollow at the base of her neck.

She tips her head back and laughs. But I notice the tension in her shoulders. The way she carries herself.

She knows exactly where I am—and that I'm watching. She hasn't looked at me once since the challenge. Not after the blindfold. Not after she hesitated on that platform and fell into the water. Not after I dove in after her and took her into my arms.

And the moment she took off that blindfold, when she looked up at me with those big, hypnotic eyes, I felt a tug at my heart. And deep down, I think she felt it, too. I just need more time with her. But how? It's not like I can force her to hear me out, to make her give me trust when I haven't earned it.

The sun burns across my shoulders. Sweat gathers at the base of my spine. I don't move. Then I notice Sean drift toward the women, specifically staring at the back of Lyla's head.

He's way too close.

I clock it before he even reaches her. The shift in his posture. The way he angles his body to hide the obvious bulge in his trunks. Casual, but intentional.

He leans on an elbow against the bar when she excuses herself and heads in the same direction.

When she settles in one of the seats, he slides closer. His awareness drops to her bikini-top-covered breasts when she isn't looking.

My hands curl slowly into fists.

"So Dallas, huh?" he says, initiating a conversation and flashing an easy smile. "Great city."

What riveting conversation. Now fuck off. The urge to cross the deck and "correct" him with more than just a knuckle sandwich burns hot and immediate.

She's not yours, you dumb fuck.

I curse under my breath. As much as I'd rather shield her from male prying eyes, this is a dating show. And right now, I'm the last person she wants around her. But that doesn't mean I have to like her being pursued.

Lyla turns toward him politely. Her smile is gracious, but distant. Controlled. Her shoulders square, chin lifted. She's definitely not interested.

"It is," she replies. "At least I think so since I live there." Her tone is light. Friendly.

Sean, somehow, must see her neutral response as an invitation to escalate further, because then he inches closer.

"Maybe you could show me around sometime," Sean continues, caressing a finger along her arm. "After we get out of here."

White-hot rage flares in my chest.

Fat chance in hell, asshole.

My hands curl slowly against the arms of the chair. If his hand travels anywhere lower or higher, so fucking help me, I will personally make sure he permanently wears his dick for a hat.

I start to rise from my chair, ready to punch Sean into next week, when I remember where I am. Cameras glint in the reflection of the pool like small, unblinking eyes. They're waiting; the producers, whoever will be watching this show when it airs, are expecting a dramatic reaction out of someone like me. I can't give them that, the satisfaction. Not when I still have so much ground to cover with Lyla.

Lyla continues to smile politely, as though she's not quite sure what to make of Sean's statement. "You seem very…confident."

"I am, baby." Even his flirting sounds sleazy.

"You'll have a great time with me."

She lets out a stiff laugh as she silently searches for an exit.

Sean doesn't notice, but I do.

Even though Lyla is giving him only friend vibes, he shifts closer still. His gaze drops—quick, subtle—then back up her body to her face.

The fact I can't throttle this guy is absolutely aggravating. But still, I don't move. I don't need to cross the deck to know what would happen if I did. And it'd only put more distance between us.

Lyla's trust with me right now is fractured. And giving her more reasons not to trust me would only hurt my case. If there's one thing I've learned today, it's where I stand in her eyes—She hardly believes a single word that comes out of my mouth. But at least she's arguing with me. If she didn't care about my being here, she wouldn't have given me the time of day.

I can work with that.

Now, if I could just get Sean to stop hitting on her. The longer he eye fucks her, the more it sets me on edge.

Heat presses down harder. The tile under my bare feet is slick with water when I stand, slow and deliberate, like I'm just stretching my legs.

I pretend nonchalance as I move toward them. Not directly, but enough to where I have a generous proximity to the conversation.

Close enough to step in but far enough to remain inconspicuous.

Sean smooths his hand down the small of Lyla's back as he laughs at something she says. It's light. Brief. But that doesn't stop me from seeing red.

Lyla is still for a few seconds. Frozen. It's subtle, but I notice it.

She shifts back, breaking the contact without acknowledging it.

Sean doesn't seem to notice her discomfort because he keeps talking.

"You always been in Dallas?" he asks.

"Yes." She gives him another polite smile with a nod.

"Family there?"

"Yes."

She's stonewalling him, giving only short answers. She only does that when someone is annoying her. Good to know she's not into a guy like that. All up in her business with little regard for her personal space. She deserves better...like me.

Fuck, if she were mine...

The house I bought years ago, sitting empty on the outskirts of town, says she already is. At least to me.

"Must be nice," he says. "Having something solid to go back to."

Her gaze flicks over his shoulder. Not to me. In fact, past me. And to the ocean horizon. As if she were staring off into space. "It is," she replies evenly, taking her gaze back to Sean.

Sean leans in again.

His dick is going to be a hat if he doesn't take a step back.

"You seem different today," he says with fake concern. "Quieter."

Her eyes sharpen slightly. "Do I?"

"Yeah. Like you're distracted."

Distracted. By what? By who? Would that have to do with me?

"I appreciate the concern, but I'm okay. Really. I need to get back to the girls."

She walks away from Sean before he can get another word in.

I can't help but smirk in satisfaction, watching Sean's confident expression falter.

I watch as she sits down at the edge of the pool again with the other women. Her back faces me as I sit down at a chair nearby, pretending to admire the view while subtly listening to their conversation.

Valerie watches intently. "He's not wrong, you know."

"Wrong about what?"

"You do seem distracted today."

Lyla hesitates. "*Distracted* is the wrong word. I guess you could say I'm... processing."

"I get you. That challenge was awful."

Lyla shakes her head. "It's more than that."

Valerie smirks. "So that's a no on Sean?"

"He has his...qualities, but I'm not interested," Lyla replies.

"Who is catching your eye then?"

Ain't that a great question?

Valerie seems to watch whatever expression is on Lyla's face with as much curiosity as I feel.

Across the deck, I notice one of the producers subtly adjust their position. Cameras angle in the women's and my direction. I realize I've put myself in a precarious position. Do they think I'm some brute, waiting for the opportune moment to intervene? Waiting to stake my claim?

They'd probably be right, but that's beside the point.

As much as I want to sweep her off her feet, I can't make Lyla feel something she doesn't. Not when I have my past stacked against me. But so far this information is helpful. She's confused, processing. Which means she's thinking. There could be a chance she hasn't completely shut me down, shut out the possibility of us down.

Before Lyla can answer Valerie's question, Miranda's voice cuts across the space, amplified and bright.

"Contestants! I hope everyone's enjoying the sunshine."

Groans ripple through the group.

"Because tomorrow," she continues, smiling like a cat, "we'll be testing something far more interesting than trust."

The words hang in the humid air.

Lyla's expression doesn't change, though her pulse jumps in her throat.

Miranda beams. "Be ready. It's going to be...intimate."

When Miranda makes her exit, murmurs spread. Speculation, excitement, and anxiety rolled into one.

What could be "far more interesting than trust"?

When I look back in Lyla's direction, her shoulders have dropped a fraction, and she inhales before sliding into the pool completely. Water consumes her body whole. And when she resurfaces, her hair is slicked back, droplets clinging to her lashes. She looks...relieved.

For half a second, her eyes find me.

But there's no smile behind this stare. Just that same charge that crackled between us on the obstacle course. Heat, burning need, and awareness of both.

Her gaze is fixed solely on my face before her chest rises in an inhale and she dives under again. The surface of the pool closes over her, rippling, distorting her shape.

I don't know if she's looking to escape, avoid me, preparing for what's to come, or all the above. But when she disappears beneath the water, the pressure in my chest doesn't ease. It builds.

Whatever enigma of a challenge is waiting for us tomorrow, something tells me it will only further complicate things.

Day Three

Lyla

I shouldn't have listened to him.

That's the part that won't stop replaying in my head.

Fabric over my eyes. Rope gliding across my hands. His voice, low and steady, even when my heart couldn't stop pounding in my ears.

You're going to have to trust me.

And during that challenge, I did. The worst part? It felt right, and I was drawn to follow. But at the same time, I couldn't. There was no way of knowing if I'd drop, no way of knowing he'd get me from point A to B without falling. I just kept thinking, if I could sense for myself where I needed to go, what was in front of me, I could get myself across safely. But in the end, I fell.

I spent the rest of that day and through the night, talking to the other girls. I even entertaining the idea of Sean, though his idea of a conversation was more of a booty call than anything else.

Scott must have gotten the message because he didn't say a word, either.

I ended up tossing and turning all night, restless. And when I finally woke up to the gray predawn light, I could see his silhouette. One arm flung over his eyes, the other hanging off the narrow cushions.

This is the second night he's slept on that god-awful couch and not once has he complained. I hate that I notice. Hate that the sight of him cramped and uncomfortable twists something in my chest like guilt I didn't ask for and don't owe him.

Throughout the day, I've reminded myself what he did, to not give in to lingering feelings. They're residual from a painful past and nothing more. But even so, my body still hums from yesterday. The way he'd touched me, the desperate hunger in his kiss, how easily I gave in.

His words especially keep circling like vultures that won't land until their prey has died. I can't process this. I can't make it make sense.

"Okay, but seriously," Emily says, sprawled across my bed while I pretend to organize my already-organized suitcase. "How much longer are you planning to avoid that man? We have another challenge."

"I'm not avoiding him. I'm...giving myself space."

She snorts. "That sounds exactly like someone who's avoiding their ex."

I shake my head.

"Girl," she continues. "You've practically been doing elaborate gymnastics to stay on the opposite side of whatever room he's in at any given moment. It's impressive, actually. Like watching a very attractive game of human *Pac-Man*."

I throw a bikini top to her. "Here, you can borrow this one. And I'm simply regaining leverage."

"Regaining leverage over what? You can't avoid him forever."

My stomach knots into a fist.

After yesterday, I've been furious. Not just at him but at myself. For how fast I gave in to his kiss. How much my heart fluttered when he held me close to his chest as he swam us to safety. How much afterward I felt a craving for more.

For so long, I've learned to be on my own. Sure, there were times I was lonely and gave in to the occasional date or hookup, but I took care of myself. Yet all it took for me to melt into him was a kiss. He still knows every button to push, every weak spot I have, and the fact that I gave in so completely makes me want to punch something—preferably him.

Avoiding him is the only way I can find control again. Can feel like I have power over whether this breaks me. If I let him close again, like before, I'll only be repeating history. And I refuse to make those same mistakes.

So I've been moving like I'm walking through a minefield. Pool time when he's in the gym. Breakfast and lunch positioned so other people act as buffers between us. Every strategic step is a deliberate fuck you to the part of me that still responds to him.

"There's a difference between regaining leverage and hiding," Emily says from the doorway.

"Enlighten me," I snap, folding the same shirt again, harder this time.

"If you were regaining leverage, you'd be facing him head-on, setting boundaries, taking the reins. Right now, you're just pretending he doesn't still have the upper hand."

"For such a confident, intense man, he's being very patient," she adds.

"How do you mean?"

"I've seen him try to approach you at least a dozen times in the last two days."

"That's the problem." I sink onto the bed beside her. "He's being... perfect. Respectful. Giving me space."

Emily frowns. "Why is that bad? With what you've been saying, it sounds like that's exactly what you want."

"Because I don't know what to do with it," I say honestly. "There's no changing what happened. But I also can't move on with him and pretend the past doesn't exist."

"So you're avoiding him because you're scared of what happens if you don't? If you let him in?"

I let out a short, controlled breath. "I'm avoiding him because I know exactly what happens if I let him too close. I'll lose myself and get hurt in the process once he's done with me."

"How do you know that will happen?"

"Because it has before."

"But you were teenagers, right? I highly doubt he's the same person now as he was then."

"That doesn't change the memories I have of hurting and crying myself to sleep."

Emily drops her shoulders, sitting up from the bed. "You're right, it doesn't. But if I were you, I'd be curious to know why he left."

"The point is moot."

"I wouldn't be so sure about that. An explanation would at least give you closure. Has he offered one?"

"Kind of? He's waiting for when it's just us, whenever that is, to give me an explanation."

"Just you guys? That's something you don't hear every day around here."

"How so? I think that just sounds like an excuse to delaying the obvious ghosting excuse."

"If he'd just ghosted, he would have been nonchalant about coming here. No. Whatever he has to say to you, it has to be very important. Maybe even life-altering."

I shake my head. "Maybe so, but the thing is I don't know if I'm ready to hear any explanation from him. Quite frankly, I don't know if I even want to."

"Don't shoot me, but from what I've seen since we got here, I think there's still a connection between you and him."

"A connection?" I can hardly believe her words. "The only connection there still is between us is his guilt."

"If he only felt guilt, he would've just said his peace to you over the phone, not follow you onto a dating show. He's here for a reason. And it's much bigger than some apology or an excuse for the past. More than I think you're willing to admit."

"He walked out once. One day he was there, and the next he was gone. No warning. No explanation. I barely survived. I don't know if I can risk going through that kind of heartbreak twice."

Emily takes my hand, looking over at me. "I get you, but you're bracing for something he hasn't done yet."

Before I can respond, a production assistant's voice carries through the villa.

"Attention, contestants! Pool deck in one hour for today's challenge and afterwards a special announcement!"

Emily and I exchange looks.

"That doesn't sound ominous at all," I mutter with sarcasm.

"From what I know about other shows, announcements mean one of two things," Emily exclaims. "A rule change that ups the stakes...or new people."

Fresh drama or fresh blood. I can't tell which one is worse.

"Regardless, though," I say, "new people tend to bring drama with them, intentionally or otherwise."

"Fair point," she agrees.

Despite the lack of control there is in this environment, from now on, I will cling to the one thing I still can control: avoiding Scott Bennett while I still can.

"Actually," Emily says slowly, like she's turning something over in her head, "this might not be the worst thing to happen."

I shoot her a look. "Do I even want to ask?"

Emily shrugs. "You're on a dating show. New people showing up might...shift the energy."

I stare at her. "You're suggesting I—what?—distract myself with these new people? Not exactly helpful if they're the same gender as us."

"I'm suggesting that if it's a man, and an attractive one at that, someone you think you could get along with, you could simply...divert your attention to them. Expand your options. Your world doesn't have to revolve around Scott."

Open myself up to someone else? Get to know them? Explore a different connection while Scott watches? The feeling in the pit of my stomach grows. Not out of guilt but nerves.

Let him see me move on. Let him watch me smile at someone else, laugh at someone else's jokes.

"Wouldn't that make him jealous? I'm already doing that...kind of."

"Definitely, but I think you could use better options than what's here. I heard you turned down Sean."

I wince. "Let's just say it wasn't going to work out."

"I don't blame you. Neither would Valerie. She said he can come off a bit...strong."

We both laugh.

But then I shake my head. "I don't want to use someone else to provoke my ex. That wouldn't be fair to them if they had feelings for me."

"You wouldn't be using anyone. If you like whoever catches your eye, you should explore that. You'd just be reminding Scott he doesn't get automatic access anymore."

My pulse skips.

What am I doing? This is crazy—and low-key a bad idea.

But I at least have to try.

"And if it helps... Yesterday, when you went to go change for dinner, Sean asked Scott if you guys were still serious, and he snapped a deck chair in half right in front of him. Scared the shit out of Sean."

I gasp.

He did that?

"That's insane."

"Call it what you want, but that man looks at you like you're oxygen."

Heat curls and pulls tight, traveling low in my belly, and I suddenly feel hot all over.

No. Bad Lyla. A man breaking furniture isn't sexy.

I shake my head, pushing whatever pull I feel down immediately.

As we head downstairs an hour later, I catch sight of Scott on the pool deck. He's talking to Bradley and Nick, but his attention goes straight to me when I make it onto the terrace.

Does he have a mental radar specifically tuned to me or something?

Seeing him steals my breath. Heat blooms in me. My heart pounds before I remember all the reasons I shouldn't feel this way.

Emily's right. I can't keep running forever. But surrendering to this without answers feels worse. Yet I'm also not sure if I'm ready for them. I need to buy myself more time.

When Miranda appears with her crew and that exploitative smile, I get the feeling that this show is about to turn on its head.

Chapter Six

Lyla

The pool deck shimmers in the afternoon light. Chlorine, salt water, and sunscreen hang heavy in the air. The producers have rearranged the loungers into a circle like we're about to hold hands and sing "Kumbaya." Not emotionally dismantle each other or rather make idiots of ourselves on cable television.

Miranda stands at the edge of the pool in a white romper that looks like it probably costs more than my rent.

"Everyone's here? Good." She looks around at all of us contestants. Half are on one side of the circle, while the rest are on the other half. Scott is across from me, controlled, observant.

The moment his stare meets mine, I look away.

"Then I think we're ready to start rolling," Miranda informs the crew behind the camera.

"Alright, rolling," a producer yells.

Immediately, Miranda's seeming slow smile forms tightly on her face. "Contestants! Welcome to our second challenge. Now, this one is where we'll get more...up close and personal."

My stomach tightens. What does that mean?

She goes on. "Today is about testing something far more than just trust: chemistry. Instinct. Natural desires. You will all be in this very circle blindfolded. When I tap your shoulder, that will be your cue to remove said blindfold—and to kiss one person within the circle."

My stomach drops. Not because of what the challenge entails, but because I know exactly how it will go. Because of Scott.

Heat crawls up my neck. My pulse kicks up before I even look over at him.

He looks intrigued, almost amused. He arches a brow toward me.

I tear my gaze away.

Don't react. Don't give him or them anything.

Miranda continues. "Everyone else will remain blindfolded while you make your decision. And you will remain anonymous to whoever you kiss. You can either choose the person you're coupled up with or whoever has piqued your interest. The choice is up to you."

Murmurs ripple through the group.

"Once you've made your choice, and given your smooches, you'll return to your spot in the circle and put your blindfold back on. When everyone has had a turn, you'll be given a signal to take off your blindfolds, ending the challenge. Sound simple?" Miranda pauses as though for dramatic effect, given the sly smirk on her face. "But be warned. Every action...has its consequence. Especially when everyone can hear you."

Moments later, we're each given thick blindfolds.

A producer appears with her tablet in hand, going around to each contestant. At one point, she stops at Scott.

"You," she points to him, "can you look more brooding? Maybe clench your fists and jaw?"

I am shocked at the woman's words. Scott's expression, along with his voice, turns cold. "You want me to perform my emotions for your cameras?"

"Think of it as...enhancing the narrative." Shockingly, the sharp producer seems unfazed.

"It's manipulation. Now fuck off."

I can't help but let out a small laugh.

"Yeah, that's perfect. More of that. Thanks." The producer then walks off.

"Everyone, please put your blindfolds on," Miranda instructs, "and we will begin."

I tie my blindfold behind my head. The world instantly swallows me into darkness, leaving me with my thundering heart. The fabric presses against my lashes. The scent of chlorine sharpens with my hearing. Someone laughs nervously, while another nearby shifts on their feet.

I breathe in through my nose and out through my mouth, trying to stay calm as footsteps move around me.

What could go wrong? I already know how this will play out. Scott will kiss me, maybe someone else, but that's a stretch, and then it'll be over.

My only concern currently is who I will choose to kiss. On the one hand, Scott is familiar, but that would only further complicate how I feel about him. Choosing someone else, however—someone I don't have any emotional ties to—would be the easy way out but could easily backfire on me if I don't choose the right person. Then again, it could fire up Scott, regardless. It'd have to be someone Scott doesn't find threatening but who I don't think I could form any attachment to.

The first selection must have been made because I hear tentative footsteps, then the soft, wet sounds of lips meeting.

My stomach churns. I feel like I've walked in on a couple's make-out session.

We're all standing here, forced to listen to each other kiss, well, each other. For those not affected emotionally, it's invasive. But for those who are... I can't imagine the humiliation they must or will be feeling or the fallout that's taking place, and what's to come, beyond my blindfold.

I hear more footsteps. They're getting distant. Not knowing what's happening, who's finished or beginning, is driving me nuts.

Then I hear kissing close to my right. This sounds hungry. Someone moans. If I remember correctly, Valerie was standing to my right. That could be her. The question is, who's kissing her?

I fold my arms around myself, holding tight like that might keep me from falling apart or, better yet, help me disappear.

I flinch slightly when I feel a light tap on my shoulder.

My pulse spikes.

My turn? Already?

I slide the blindfold off my face, blinking against the sudden sunlight. Eleven people stand frozen around me, eyes covered. I can't help but look over at Scott. Solid. Still. As if anticipating what's to come. The rigidness in his posture, the barely contained storm he holds back in his presence.

The longer I stare, the more I realize how easy it'd be to just take the short step forward, reach for him, and give in to his kiss again. Just thinking about it makes me melt. But, choosing him would only open another can of worms I'm not ready to confront. Would only confirm what he believes about me, about us. That there's still a chance after so long apart.

I'm not going to give him the upper hand.

I move carefully as my gaze slides past him and to the other male contestants. But only one of them makes the most sense to me in this situation. Sure it might piss off Kylie, but I don't have much choice but to choose Zayne.

He is attractive in his own right as well as fun to be around, but that's not the reason why I'm choosing him. I'm kissing him because he's the safe choice, an easy choice. I have no history with him; he's uncomplicated. As far as I know, he hasn't given Scott any reason to hate him. I also have no romantic feelings for him. On top of that, because he's on a completely different end of the circle as Scott, Zayne will never know it was me, and Scott won't know who I kissed instead of him.

I cross the circle on unsteady legs, acutely aware of Scott going rigid at the corner of my eyes. But I keep going.

I barely give Zayne time to react—or myself time to lose my nerve—before I lean in and kiss him with a gentle touch to his lips.

Yeah, he's not for me.

The guy knows what he's doing, the pressure is right, and the angle practiced. He tastes like spearmint and simplicity. But there's no pull. No spark. Nothing in me reaches, much less craves, for more.

It's like kissing a polite stranger. Which is exactly what I need.

When I pull back, the emptiness is immediate and cold. I leave him where he stands and walk back to my place in the circle before putting the blindfold back over my eyes.

Darkness quickly envelops me again.

The game continues as I hear soft but distant laughter to my left. That's quickly followed by more shuffling, a sharp inhale, and then faint sounds of moans and kisses.

Sometime later, deliberate footsteps approach—slow, measured, like the owner has all night and nowhere else he'd rather be. The air warms, thickens. A big body settles right in front of me, close enough that his heat reaches out and brushes my skin before anything else does.

Whoever he is, he chose me.

My spine straightens. Is it Scott?

Large, rough hands settle on my waist—warm, solid, fingers spreading wide. The grip is firm but patient, no rush, no shake. He draws me in slowly until my breasts press against the hard wall of his chest. Tall. Broad. Nothing but dense muscles under the fabric. Solid in a way that makes my breath hitch.

He doesn't feel like Scott.

My palms slide up thick forearms, over wide shoulders, mapping unfamiliar ridges and planes. Everything is new. Foreign. My pulse skips at the sheer strangeness of it—someone who doesn't already know every scar and fault line.

His hands move without hesitation. They glide up my sides, trace the length of my arms, then—slow, deliberate—cup my face. Thumbs brush my cheekbones like he's memorizing the shape of me. Like time belongs to him.

Then his mouth covers mine.

I flinch slightly at the sudden contact, but he stays. The kiss begins soft, restrained. Warm lips press with quiet certainty, not tentative, not devouring. Just... sure.

He tastes like aged whiskey and the darkest chocolate—rich, lingering, slow burning,—coating my tongue. A low rumble vibrates from his chest into mine, satisfied, almost pleased.

One hand slides into my hair, fingers threading deep at the roots, tilting me exactly where he needs me. The other hand settles at the small of my back, broad palm pressing me closer until there's no air between us. He anchors me there, like I might float away if he lets go.

The kiss deepens—unhurried, confident. His tongue traces the seam of my lips once, patient, coaxing. When I part for him, he slips inside slowly. Exploring. Tasting with no frantic claim, just deliberate strokes that make heat coil low in my belly despite myself. He knows what he's doing. Every tilt, every gentle suck on my lower lip, every soft glide of tongue is precise, practiced. The kind of skill that usually melts thought into nothing.

My fingers curl into his shoulders, gripping hard. My body leans in —instinct, not choice—chasing the slow burn.

He's good. Devastatingly good. But something is missing.

I feel it like a shadow under the pleasure. No spark of recognition. No shared history. This is clean. Easy. A perfect stranger who knows nothing about the wreckage inside me.

This should feel like freedom. Instead, it feels...empty.

When he finally eases back, his lips linger for a moment. His hands slide down my arms, find my hands, lace our fingers for one suspended second. Then he lets go.

I hear footsteps retreat—unhurried, same as they came.

I stand frozen. Lips tingling, swollen. Chest heaving in shallow bursts. Skin buzzing where he touched.

Who was that?

Curiosity flickers, bright and unbidden, in my mind. But another question forms that's louder, sharper. A question that sinks into my bones.

Why does a kiss that perfect leave me feeling...nothing?

I don't have much time to fully process these questions before I hear footsteps coming at me fast—too fast. Then the scent of cedar and rain slam into me, wrapping around my lungs until my chest seizes.

Scott.

He's right there. Close enough that his heat licks my skin before he even touches me. His breathing saws, rough, uneven, like he's been running full-out. Or like he's ravenous.

"My turn," he rasps, voice scraped raw.

His hands capture my face—strong, unyielding, thumbs pressing under my jaw like he's locking me exactly where he wants me. No room to escape. No room to think.

"I need you." The words vibrate against my mouth, low and feral.

Then his lips crash into mine. Hard. Hungry. No preamble.

Everything else vanishes. The world shrinks to the brutal press of his mouth, the scrape of his five-o'clock shadow raking my chin, the way his arms band around me and yank me flush against him until I feel every rigid inch of his body molding to mine. His tongue pushes in—demanding, stroking deep—and I taste salt, heat, and something darker, something that's all him. I open wider on instinct, meeting him stroke for stroke, chasing the invasion like I'll die if I don't.

A growl rumbles in his chest. It vibrates through me, settles low in my belly, and lights me up. My fingers twist into his shirt, pulling him impossibly closer. I arch into him. My hips rolling forward until the thick, insistent ridge of him presses right where I ache most. A shock of need spears through me, sharp and sweet, and a moan tears out of my throat before I can stop it.

He answers with a rough sound, cups my face tighter, angles me so he can go deeper. His teeth catch my bottom lip—sharp enough to sting. Then his tongue soothes the bite in a slow, deliberate drag that makes my knees buckle. I whimper into his mouth, the sound swallowed by him, and everything inside me knots tighter: grief, want, years of buried ache unraveling at once.

Muscle memory takes over. My body remembers him even if my mind fights it—remembers how to tilt, how to give, how to take. I press up on my toes, chasing more, drowning in the slick heat of his tongue, the way his hands slide down to grip my waist like he'll never let go.

When he finally wrenches back, the separation rips through me like tearing flesh. Cold air hits my swollen lips. My pulse thunders in my ears, my skin buzzing, every nerve raw and alive like they were the last time we kissed.

He stays close, breath fanning my mouth. "Kiss whoever you want," he murmurs, so quiet it's only for me. "That won't change a damn thing."

Then he's gone, and I'm left trembling.

My heart slams against my ribs. My lips tingle, my body still arched toward the space where he used to be.

Why does he still wreck me like this?

"Blindfolds off, everyone!" Miranda's voice cuts sharp through the haze in my head.

I yank the cloth away and blink hard against the sudden glare. My eyes adjust in quick, stinging flashes.

The circle stares back. Zayne's grin is lazy, entertained. Emily's lips are swollen, her gaze still dazed and faraway. Valerie stands statue-still, chin high, eyes scanning every face like she's tallying points. Scott—shoulders squared, arms loose at his sides—locks eyes with me. Composed. Too composed.

Then I see them.

Two new bodies in the ring. A woman with long legs and sharp angles, radiating confidence in a sheer beach coverup over a hot pink string bikini. But it's the man beside her who stops my breath.

Light brown hair catches the sun, hazel eyes steady and knowing. A body built from discipline, not vanity. The second his gaze finds mine, my chest cinches tight.

Him. My mystery kisser.

I trace the shape of his mouth, the patient curve of his smile—the same unhurried intention I felt when those lips covered mine, slow and deliberate, like he had forever to savor. A kiss that shouldn't still echo inside me. But it does.

"Everyone, meet our wild cards—Ava and Damon," Miranda purrs. "They've been playing along in today's challenge and will be joining us as contestants."

Gasps and murmurs ripple throughout. But I can barely hear them.

Scott's stare burns at the edge of my vision—unmoving, fixed on me. Not on Damon. Just me. Like the rest of the deck dissolved.

The look steals the air from my lungs. It isn't rage but rather something quieter. Darker. Like a door swinging shut on something fragile.

Then, slowly, his mouth curves into a knowing grin.

Damn him.

"Since they're new," Miranda continues, "they each get to pick someone for a one-on-one date tonight."

Damon's eyes flick between Scott and me. Not threatened but rather curious. Assessing.

The group starts to scatter as Damon walks straight to me.

"Lyla." His voice is warm, smooth. He lifts my hand with easy confidence, pressing a slow kiss to my knuckles. The gesture surprises me. "It's nice to meet you."

"N-nice to meet you, too."

His smile deepens, like he caught the stutter in my pulse. "Would you join me for dinner tonight?"

The deck falls silent. I feel Scott before I see him—heat rolling at my back, presence sharpening every inch of space. When I glance over, he hasn't moved. But his eyes have darkened. Focused. Tracking the way Damon's fingers still curl around mine.

After Scott's kiss, the way his mouth claimed me, after his growled *I need you* still vibrates in my ears—I need air. Distance. Anything to break the pull.

I force myself to really look at Damon.

He's handsome and gives off an energy that feels safe, uncomplicated, like solid ground after years of quicksand. He's a man who makes a decision and stands by it. He's possibility.

If there's even a sliver of a chance I can move forward, build something clean and uncomplicated—something that doesn't carve me open every time—I have to take it. If saying yes to Damon creates distance from the gravitational pull Scott still exerts—yanking me back every damn time—then I need that distance.

Love can grow. With time. With deliberate choice.

I inhale, trying to steady myself.

"Yes," I whisper.

The word lands solid in my chest, anchoring me.

Scott's laugh is low, sharp, humorless, as if it were a blade wrapped in velvet. Every hair on my arms rises.

Then he moves. Not fast but deliberate. Inevitable.

He closes the gap until I can feel the heat radiating off him, until I can smell the faint salt of his skin and the dark edge of his musk. His hand captures my wrist—firm, unyielding, unmistakably possessive.

The deck around us goes eerily quiet, like the world is holding its breath for this moment.

He doesn't look at Damon. Only me.

His voice drops to gravel and smoke, pitched for my ears only. "Don't forget you were in my arms five minutes ago, little one."

His grip tightens around my wrist. Not enough to cause pain but to certainly get the message across that he isn't exactly thrilled. My skin flushes hot, traitorous heat pooling low in my belly. For one unguarded heartbeat, something feral flashes in his eyes—raw hunger, sharp dislike, almost jealousy, and a flicker of pain—before he schools his expression. His jaw flexes. Every muscle coils like he's two seconds from dragging me against him and claiming what he thinks is still his.

He holds my stare another punishing second before letting go. "Enjoy your date." His voice is smooth, almost polite.

But his eyes are anything but. They're black fire, locked on me, promising. And that promise trails down my spine, a shiver I can't suppress.

For one moment, the air turns syrup thick, suffocating.

Then—

"Hey, Lyla."

Emily's voice cuts through, artificially bright, like we're debating drink orders instead of witnessing this detonation.

"Can you come help me with sunscreen?"

The tension fractures just enough for me to feel like I can breathe again.

I nod, grateful, and let her loop her arm through mine, already pulling me down the stairs, toward the pool deck below.

Behind us, the tension doesn't disappear. It coils tighter. Waiting. And deep in my gut, I know with bone-deep certainty this isn't close to finished.

Scott

The second Lyla breathes *yes* to Damon's invitation, something in my chest doesn't crack. It fucking detonates.

She's going on a date with him.

After the way she melted against me—lips parting, body arching, that soft, greedy sound she makes when she's already half-gone.

I turn and stalk away before the instinct to drag her back into my arms overrides every shred of sense. Before I give the cameras something explosive—and irreversible.

The gym is blessedly empty.

Perfect.

I can't touch her right now. Can't fix this mess with my hands or my mouth the way every screaming cell in my body demands. So I wrap my knuckles, the tape biting into skin, and channel it all into the heavy bag.

I start slow. Controlled.

Then faster. Harder.

Crack.

Her choice echoes in my skull. Damon's cool certainty, the way he looked at her like he already owned the space beside her in bed.

Crack.

I know he kissed her during the challenge. He wouldn't have asked her otherwise. But did she make that same breathless little moan—the one that has my cock stand at attention?

Crack.

I slam harder than I should. Pain shoots up my arm, bright and welcome, yanking me out of this mental spiral.

"Fuck," I snarl, the word ripping out.

I brace my forehead against the bag, chest heaving, forcing the beast within back under. This is a dating show. She's supposed to explore options. As she fucking should. But logic doesn't stop my blood from boiling at the thought of his hands on her. His mouth. His anything.

I can't fight this the caveman way—not without torching my shot. Not without ruining my chance at getting Lyla to hear the truth. I have to play their game. Rebuild the trust I shattered. Prove I'm not a man she can't just love, but also rely on, again.

I straighten, my jaw locked so tight my teeth ache.

As much as I'd love to tell this Damon guy to fuck off, I can't. So for now, I'm punching this bag—and imagining it was him.

The gym door creaks open behind me. Footsteps quickly follow.

I don't turn immediately. When I do, Damon's framed in the doorway like he owns the fucking villa.

The sleeves of his dress shirt are rolled to his elbows. His hair slicked back. Hands in his pockets. He's calm, almost nonchalant.

"Quite the healthy outlet," he observes, voice smooth as silk over steel.

I roll my shoulders, crack my neck. "Got something to say?"

He steps inside, letting the door click shut—soft, deliberate. The sound lands like a gauntlet.

"She said yes to dinner." His statement is flat. Factual. As if I didn't watch the whole goddamn thing.

I stay silent.

He tilts his head. "And the entire time, she was fighting not to look at you. Even after the word left her mouth."

"You got the date," I grit out. "What's your point?"

"Something's been nagging at me." He meets my eyes—cool, assessing. Calculating. "You're the ex, aren't you?"

I don't deny it.

He nods once, like the final puzzle piece snapped in. "That explains…everything."

"Explains what?" I lower my voice an octave, bracing.

He doesn't rush. Just studies me, no doubt measuring whether this conversation is worth the risk of my fist.

"You overwhelm her," he says finally. "That's exactly why she said yes to me. Because I'm not you."

My next breath is razor-thin.

"So what? You think playing the safe, chill guy automatically wins you brownie points?" The words come out rough-edged.

"I think she wants to know what it feels like to breathe around someone who doesn't make her feel like she's one wrong move from destruction." He shrugs. "Someone who doesn't crowd her the way you do."

I take a single furious step forward, closing the gap until I can smell his cologne—clean, expensive, nothing like the sweat and heat I want to bury myself in with her.

He doesn't flinch. Doesn't tense. Just holds my stare.

"You've had one staged kiss and not even five minutes of conversation," I growl, voice scraping gravel. "You don't know her."

Not the way her pulse jumps under my thumb. Not the sounds she makes in her sleep.

"No," he agrees, infuriatingly even. "But I will. And I'm looking forward to every second of learning her."

I curl my hands into fists at my sides. The urge to slam him into the wall—to wipe that smug, calm certainty off his face has— me on edge.

He turns toward the door. "She deserves someone who doesn't make her wait for the other shoe to drop."

I'm about ready to snap this fucker like a twig.

He glances back, eyes sharp as a blade. Then he's gone.

I stand there, tape creaking, pulse a slow, dangerous drum.

Every instinct screams to find her, pin her to the nearest wall, and remind her exactly how right we are. How she fits so perfectly in my life. How no one else will ever touch that place inside my heart that only she can open.

But I don't move. Because the bastard's right about one thing. She said yes.

I hate it, but she only said yes to dinner. Not forever.

So when she walks back from her date with him—flushed, conflicted, maybe even a little guilty from whatever polite spark he tried to ignite—I'll be waiting. And this time, I won't let logic stop me from showing her every filthy, tender reason she should be mine.

Chapter Seven

Lyla

The private cabana table is set for romance.

White linen, low candles, the ocean glittering like shattered glass under the moon. The chef's tasting menu arrives in perfect waves. From citrus-seared scallops, to chilled lobster tail dripping beurre blanc, to mango sorbet that melts too fast on my tongue. Damon is attentive without being smothering. He asks real questions—about the wedding I just pulled off with the ripped bustle, about how I built Clark Events with a laptop and determination. He listens. Actually listens.

He's safe. Steady. Logical.

And I hate that every polite smile I give him feels like a performance.

Not just because that hollowness I feel in my chest won't go away. But also because Scott is watching.

I can feel him from fifty yards away, up on the main villa deck where the rest of the contestants are pretending to drink cocktails and not stare. His gaze is a physical thing—hot, unblinking, sliding over my bare shoulders, down the silk of my dress where it clings to my waist, lingering on the curve of my thigh crossed over the other. My nipples pebble against the thin fabric. Heat coils low in my belly, insistent and humiliating. My thighs press together under the table.

Focus on Damon. Get it together, girl.

Damon leans forward, refilling my wine. His fingers brush mine. Warm. Careful. Nothing like the rough, claiming way Scott used to slide his palm up my thigh.

"You're quiet tonight," he says. His voice is gentle but direct.

I force a smile. "Just taking it all in. It's beautiful here."

He tilts his head, studying me, as though he's collecting data.

"It is. But beauty's cheap. Compatibility is what's most important." He sets the bottle down. "Okay, now I have to know. You must have other stories about being a wedding planner."

A laugh escapes before I can stop it. "You want to know all the gory details?"

"I want to know everything," he replies with intent.

"Okay." His stare on me makes it hard to focus at first. "I once had a groom's mother release doves during the ceremony. I specifically told her not to, and she did it anyway—without telling anyone, including the bride and groom. Sure enough, one of the birds flew straight into the minister's face."

"No." His eyes widen, delighted.

"Yes," I wince. "Mid-vow. The bride was screaming, guests were ducking, and I stood there trying to herd panicked birds out of a chapel with a broom." I shake my head, smiling despite myself. "The photographer got the most amazing shot, though. Pure chaos but absolutely worth it."

Damon laughs—warm, genuine, the kind that makes the corners of his eyes crinkle. "That's incredible. Did the couple survive it?"

"They thought it was hilarious once the shock wore off and they realized no one was hurt. Sent me a bottle of wine last Christmas."

My shoulders ease, the tightness I hadn't noticed slipping away into the warm night air.

"See, that's what I don't understand about weddings," he says, gesturing with his fork. "People spend thousands of dollars chasing perfect, and somehow the disaster becomes the memory that sticks."

"It's the imperfection," I say, surprised by how easily the words come. "Perfect is boring. And it almost never exists."

His smile lingers, but there's something sharper underneath it.

"Maybe I should come watch you work sometime. See the method behind the madness."

"Maybe."

The conversation keeps flowing—easy, weightless. Damon makes me laugh with quick, dry humor that lands effortlessly, without history attached.

"I can't imagine doing what you do," he says. "It must be either incredibly romantic...or completely exhausting."

"Both," I admit. "Some couples are real fairy tales. Others..." I shrug. "Let's just say I've talked more than one bride off a proverbial ledge."

He smiles at that. "And yet you keep doing it."

"I guess I do."

"Most people would've burned out by now." His gaze is thoughtful, not probing. "Or stopped believing in it altogether."

"You say that like you have."

"Not exactly." He pauses, considering. "I just don't chase the big, dramatic version of things anymore."

"You seem cynical."

He chuckles softly. "*Practical*, is the term I'd use."

The word settles between us. Solid. Reasonable, but...cold.

His fingers brush mine as he reaches for his glass—brief, unassuming. The contact is easy but not electric.

That's the thing. It doesn't unsettle me. Doesn't spark or linger. It's simply as it is. That should come as a relief, but it doesn't. Why is that? I should have my head examined.

He leans back, relaxed. "I like knowing where I stand. I've found things tend to last longer when you don't ask them to be everything."

I nod, even though something in my chest tightens.

After dinner, he gestures toward the shoreline. "Walk with me?"

Moments later, the sound of the waves fills the quiet between us. The calm stays, but the absence has weight. Like I've forgotten something but can't name what.

"Can I ask you something?" Damon says as we walk along the water's edge.

"Sure."

He hesitates, eyes on the horizon. "You and Scott... I'm getting the sense that chapter's not closed yet."

It's not a question. Not really.

"We were together in high school," I say. "First love." I keep it light. Surface level. "Then he left without explanation. That about sums it up."

Damon studies me for a moment, expression thoughtful, not prying.

"I see," he says.

I don't answer.

He doesn't push.

Instead, he slows his pace, giving me space without stepping away. "I like knowing what I'm walking into," he adds. "Not because I need everything spelled out— I just don't like surprises."

Scott was, and continues to be, a surprise.

Damon continues before I can linger on the thought. "I had a similar experience. The kind of love that takes over your whole life." He exhales slowly, eyes fixed on the horizon. "Let's just say it cost more than it gave."

I almost ask what he means, but something in his tone—the flat finality—tells me not to.

We walk in silence for a few steps, the water curling around our ankles.

"What if I don't want just compatibility?" The question slips out before I can stop it.

He looks at me then—not pitying. Not judging. Just honest.

"Then I'd tell you to be careful about handing your heart to someone who's already burned you once," he says.

The words land softly. Not a warning but not a promise either. Just something stated and left there between us.

His words linger, unsettling instead of reassuring, as I try to decide whether the quiet is relief—or just unfamiliarity.

Damon's hand rests lightly at the small of my back—not possessive, not demanding. Just there.

How little it affects me is hard not to notice. No restless heat. No pull. No urge to close the distance and disappear into him.

With Damon, everything stays contained. Pleasant. Easy. Safe.

I tell myself that's the point. That this is what it's supposed to feel like when something isn't complicated or dangerous.

So why do I keep waiting for—no, wanting—more?

Chapter Eight

Scott

I've welded myself to this deck railing since the torches ignited. The infinity pool spills liquid moonlight toward the black ocean below. Their table perches at the edge—candle flames dancing across Lyla's bare shoulders, silk dress shifting like water over the skin I still map in my sleep.

Damon's voice drifts up, low and even. She laughs at something he says. Soft. Polite. Nothing like the wrecked, gasping sound she made yesterday when my mouth was on her throat and her leg locked around me.

My fingers dig into the teak. Wood groans.

Moments that feel like forever pass when they stand from their table. He offers his arm like a gentleman. And she slips her hand through his forearm.

They drift down the path to the beach, sand silvered by the moon. Waves hush against their feet. His shadow bleeds into hers. She tilts her head, listening, her pale lavender hair, a striking contrast from the golden color she had before I left, catches in the breeze.

The image of them close together knives straight through my gut. Those hips were mine—nails carving half-moons into my shoulders, her whispering against my ear like a prayer only I could answer. She used to ignite me like that. Now she's giving polite smiles and taking a stroll with a man she's just met.

But she isn't mine. This is a dating show.

This is fucking torture.

"Breaking the wood isn't going to help," Bradley mutters, eyeing my white knuckles.

I don't answer.

"It's called a date, Bennett," he adds, smirking. "Some of us let them breathe longer than twenty minutes."

I lock my jaw. Breathe? She's walking away with him. And every step is carving into me another reason I should break the rules, cross the sand, and remind her exactly who she still burns for.

Bradley continues, oblivious. "Would it be so terrible if they actually got along?"

I'm two seconds from snapping his neck if he doesn't shut the fuck up.

Every inch Damon has touched is ground I claimed first. Every polite laugh she gave him tonight is an echo of sounds she made for me—raw, desperate, mine. The thought isn't logical. It's territorial. Primal. A low burn in my blood that no amount of discipline can smother.

"I know you care for her," Bradley says, softer now, "but you've got to let her figure this out. You don't strike me as the guy who'd steamroll her boundaries or her choices."

He's right. I'd cut my own hands off before I ever forced her. That doesn't stop the rage coiling tighter as I watch them disappear into the moonlight.

Until today's challenge, until Damon popped up like a fucking jack in the box, I believed I had time. Time to chip away at the wall she built against me after I left. Time to earn one civil conversation. Now it feels like we're back at day one of filming.

He claps my shoulder. "So...what's the plan, Bennett?"

I don't answer. My eyes stay locked on the beach path.

They're returning. Then Lyla pauses, murmurs something to Damon, words too quiet for me to catch against the roaring waves of the ocean. She slips away alone.

Her gaze flicks up. Toward the deck. Toward me. Her expression isn't filled with guilt; nor is it defiant. But rather unsteady, like she's caught in the same current I am.

Is she ending the date early? I have to know.

I'm already moving, my steps silent on teak, pulse a steady hammer in my throat. She takes the palm-lined path, torchlight sliding gold over bare shoulders I used to kiss until she trembled. I follow, slowly closing the distance the way I was trained to track the enemy; patient and inevitable.

I head down the stairs, my bare feet quiet on teak, pulse hammering in my throat. She takes the winding path through the palms. I follow. Not rushing. Letting the distance close naturally.

"You look beautiful tonight, little one," I say, my voice low. Just for her.

She stiffens but doesn't turn to face me. "Don't."

I stay planted. Don't step closer. "I know you're on a date, but I had to see you."

She stops. "Why follow me to the bathroom? Why watch us like that?"

"Because every time you glance back, it looks like you're waiting for me to stop pretending I'm okay with this."

She scoffs. "You're seeing things."

"I know you, Lyla. I know what disinterest looks like on you. And that"—I gesture to the expression filled with something like apprehension and longing—"that's not it."

Her brows knit. "Damon—"

"Is not for you."

She whirls; her breath hitches, sharp, eyes wide with fury, cheeks flushed. Torchlight hits the rapid rise and fall of her chest, silk pulling tight over peaked nipples. Thighs shift, press together once.

Gorgeous.

"You're interrupting my date, so I'd appreciate it if you let me get back to the table."

"Not yet."

She tries to step past. I catch her forearms, gentle but firm, and turn her to face me, holding her there just long enough for her pulse to hammer under my thumbs. Then I release her, dropping my hands to my sides.

"When are you going to admit he's not the one you want touching you?" My gaze falls to her mouth, then lower. Slow. Deliberate. "Or tell me you still don't want this"—I gesture between us—"and to walk away from you for good. Your choice."

Her lips part in a tiny gasp.

"I chose him tonight," she whispers.

"I know."

"He's a good guy."

"*Good* doesn't make your breath hitch like that. Doesn't make you shake when I'm this close."

She fists her hands. "This is my first date with Damon. You don't get to—"

"I don't get to do a lot when it comes to you. But I get to remember every night I lay awake, picturing, thinking, of you. Every night here, watching you fight this. Imagining you furious, aching, still mine."

Her eyes search mine. Shock slices through the anger. Heat climbs her neck, tangled with questions.

Silence falls between us.

I drag a hand over my jaw with a rough exhale. "Go back to him. Let him try to kiss you goodnight, if that's what it takes to lie to yourself."

I lean in just enough for my breath to brush her ear.

"But later, when you're alone in our bed, sheets twisted around your legs, hand slipping down because the ache won't let you sleep... It won't be his name on your mind."

Her knees buckle a fraction before she catches herself.

I step back. Give her the space she demands.

"Go," I say quietly. "Before I break every rule I've set and carry you upstairs myself."

She turns. Walks away on unsteady legs, hips swaying like they know my grip.

I melt back into the shadows, watching her return to the table. Damon waits—patient, composed.

Forcing a smile, she sits across from him.

I'm not leaving, little one. Not this time.

Chapter Nine

Lyla

The terrace lights fade behind me as I slip through the villa doors, Damon's polite *good night, Lyla* still echoing in my ears like white noise. I force one last smile over my shoulder—tight, practiced—then let it drop the second I'm out of his view.

My legs threaten to come out from under me. Every step down the corridor pulls at the low ache Scott left behind on that torch-lit path. His voice is still there, low and deliberate in my head. *Later, alone in our shared room, when the ache drives your hand between your thighs, it won't be Damon's name you'll think of.*

I hate that I let his words get to me.

The hallway air is cooler as the air-conditioning hits. But it does nothing to settle the heat crawling under my skin. My dress clings in places I wish it wasn't after the humid walk back.

When I arrive at the shared suite, I notice the door is ajar. Soft golden light spills into the corridor.

He's awake.

I pause at the threshold, fingers curling around the knob until my knuckles ache. My heart slams against my ribs like it wants out.

I push open the door wider. Scott stands on the balcony, back to me, forearms braced on the railing. Moonlight cuts sharp across his shoulders, rolled sleeves exposing the corded forearms I traced when we kissed yesterday morning.

The ocean rolls back and forth, restless below. He doesn't turn at the sound of the door. Doesn't speak, as though he's been waiting.

I step fully inside and close the door. The lock clicks—too loud, too final.

He turns then. Slow. Intentional. Eyes dark in the low light, unreadable except for the flicker of something raw when they lock on mine.

"How was your date?" The question sounds calm. Almost casual. But the edge underneath could slice bone.

Who the hell asks their ex about a date with someone else? This island is a goddamn fever dream.

The room shrinks until there's nothing but the space between us.

His gaze drops—traces the way my dress clings to damp skin, lingers on the rise and fall of my chest like he's memorizing every breath I'm trying to hide. When those blue eyes snap back to mine, heat flares, dark and restrained.

I cross my arms—half coverage, half armor. "Not that it's any of your business, but it was lovely. Damon is easy company. A gentleman. He actually asked about my business and listened. He's...caring."

Scott scoffs, one brow arching. "Caring." The word drips like acid. "You describe him like he's the fucking neighborhood dog—reliable, doesn't bite, easy to walk."

"I'm sorry, I don't remember asking for your permission to tell me what you think about my choices."

"I don't need your fucking permission to tell you when you're making shitty ones." His voice is low, rough. "You know damn well why I care. I can't—I won't—stand here and watch you settle for someone else just because he isn't me."

I plant my hands on my hips. "You don't know what I want anymore. You haven't for ten years. Complain all you want. It changes nothing."

His eyes lock on mine like he's looking straight through every wall I rebuilt. For a second, the air feels too thin.

"It's been a long day." I rip my gaze away. "I'm not doing this."

"You looked up at me when I was on that terrace," he says quietly. "Even with him right there, giving you every ounce of his attention, your eyes still found me."

Heat crawls up my throat. "Don't flatter yourself. I was looking around the villa."

He steps inside and closes the glass doors. The soft click lands like clock turning.

"You're a terrible liar, little one."

"I'm done." I step a step toward the bathroom—escape.

He doesn't lunge. He simply turns, controlled and deliberate, putting his body between me and the door without touching me.

"Done?" That low voice drops another octave. "That kiss today told me a different story. Both of them did."

Heat floods low in my belly, traitorous and instant. "One was a moment of weakness; the other—"

"Both were the only honest fucking thing that's happened between us since we got here." He exhales, jaw tight. "Damon seems like a good guy. Straightforward. Safe. He'll never raise his voice, never push you too hard, never make you feel anything that scares you."

I lift my chin. "Sounds perfect."

"No." He closes the last step. His body heat rolls over me, his lips inches from mine. "Deep down, you don't want Mr. Perfect. You want the man who makes you burn."

His voice is rough velvet, and it drags a shiver straight down my spine.

"I've been giving you space," he continues, breath brushing my neck. "I've been patient as hell, respecting the ten goddamn years since I last had you in my arms. But watching you smile at him tonight—" A muscle jumps in his jaw. "It fucking gutted me."

I should move. Tell him to stop. But I'm frozen, my core tightening at the raw honesty in his voice.

"I can't be him, Lyla." His hands settle lightly on my forearms—warm, steady, burning through my skin. "I can't promise easy. I can't promise comfortable. But I can promise you everything else—every dark, intense, consuming thing we used to be. And more."

"You left once," I whisper, hating how broken it sounds. "Why should I believe you won't again?"

His thumbs stroke once, slow and deliberate. "I hated every second of it. I've spent years trying to get back to a place where I could stand in front of you without dragging danger behind me. Things are different now. And I'd rather die than walk away again."

The words land like stones in still water. Stark. Honest. Dangerous.

Tears sting my eyes. This version of Scott—restrained, lethal, stripped raw—is much more dangerous than the boy I fell for.

His hands, his body, his mouth— They're right there. I can see the silver flecks in his eyes, smell the cedar-and-musk scent that's purely him. For one fractured second, my mind flashes to white walls and the echo of a heartbeat...things he doesn't know I lost. Things I swore I'd never let him near again.

He lifts one hand, thumb tracing my bottom lip with agonizing slowness. "I'm not going to stand by and watch you settle because you think it feels safe."

"I don't care what you do," I manage, but it comes out too thin, too breathless.

A ghost of a smile touches his mouth—there and gone in half a second. "Yes, you do."

For one heartbeat, I think he's going to kiss me. Every muscle in my body coils tight, waiting.

Then he steps back—slow, deliberate—leaving cold air and roaring silence in his wake.

My lungs release a shaky breath.

"It's late." His voice is calm again, command wrapped in velvet. "Get ready for bed."

He turns toward the balcony doors, giving me his back—broad, tense, every line screaming the same restraint I'm fighting not to break.

I stand there, pulse thundering, skin too tight, body still screaming for the fire he just walked away from.

Chapter Ten

Day Four

Lyla

"You look like you got hit by a truck," Emily says, sliding onto the stool beside me at the breakfast bar. Steam curls from her coffee mug.

"Thanks. Exactly the vibe I was going for," I deadpan.

"I'm serious." She nudges my shoulder. "You've been staring at that toast like it owes you money. Talk to me."

Where do I even start?

The villa buzzes around us—laughter, clinking plates, gossip about today's challenge. Everyone else is already neck-deep in their drama. I'm still replaying last night. Damon's respectful questions, his steady gaze, the complete absence of chaos. Nice. Safe. And Scott's voice in the dark afterward, low and ruthless, promising I'd ache for him when I was alone. And our argument last night had me awake all night.

Scott wasn't in the suite when I awoke. The couch hadn't been slept on; only the faint cedar scent lingered on the pillows. The hollow that carved open in my chest the second I realized he was gone scared me more than his presence ever had. Why does his absence still feel like a missing limb when my head knows better?

"Earth to Lyla." Renee appears with her own mug. "Emily asked you a question."

"Sorry. What?"

Valerie slides in across from me, brow arched. "Let me guess—the date was perfect, Damon was a gentleman, and now you're spiraling."

Is it that obvious?

"So let's be real," Valerie says gently. "How was it?"

"Great." The word slips out too easily. "We had easy conversation. He asked about my business, actually listened. He's steady—the kind of man who keeps promises."

Emily tilts her head, skeptical. "Sounds like the jackpot. So why do you look like someone just canceled Christmas?"

Because safe and easy are what I need. What I should need. A life without that terrifying, all-consuming burn might actually be the smart choice.

I exhale. "Damon gave me a lot to think about last night."

"Oh?" Emily leans in. "What kind of thinking? Dirty? Filthy?"

I lower my voice. "He makes sense. He's warm and kind. Interested in building something real and steady. I don't think he's the type to disappear when things get hard."

Valerie's eyes narrow. "That's great, but...does he light you up? Do you feel anything when he's close?"

That's the best part. I don't have to.

Before I can answer, Damon's voice slides in, warm and unruffled. "What are we talking about today, ladies?" His hand rests lightly on the back of my chair—casual, grounding.

It should feel comforting. Instead, it feels...neutral.

Exactly as it should. Practical. Safe.

Hearing rippling from the pool, I turn. Scott rises from the pool in one fluid motion, water streaming down every carved line of muscle. Dark hair slicked back, towel slung low around his neck, board shorts clinging in ways that make my mouth go dry and a traitorous ache bloom low in my belly.

He looks like he's been at war with himself all morning, coiled tension rolling off him in waves.

His gaze locks on mine. Blue. Burning. The hollow in my chest rips wider.

My pulse stutters. My skin feels hot. My carefully constructed logic wavers slightly.

And for one stupid, traitorous second, a thought pops into my mind. A thought I've denied for ten years. What if he's not bullshitting like I've been thinking he has? What if he's actually telling the truth that there's more to the story? The thought feels like betrayal—of the girl who cried alone in a hospital bed, of the woman who built an entire life so no man could ever do that again.

I shove it down hard. I'm not ready to hear whatever story he's carrying. Not yet. For all I know, I could be imagining things.

But the hollow in my chest refuses to quit.

Damon excuses himself to grab a plate. Emily leans close, whispering. "How do you feel about Scott?"

Everything.

Too much.

Not enough.

All at once.

Because no matter how much I justify, no matter how hard I try to choose the safe path, my body still screams for his fire.

Chapter Eleven

Scott

I can still feel her on my lips—not literally, but the ghost of that almost-kiss last night lingers. My thumb brushing her bottom lip, her breath catching, pupils large before I forced myself to step back. Vanilla and salt that clung to the air this morning after I left the suite early. My hands are still unsteady from not taking what she was too stubborn to give.

I'll make damn sure she knows exactly what she's walking away from.

The promise from the villa room hammers in my skull as I brace against the exterior wall, forcing my breathing to level before anyone clocks the state she's left me in. My cock is rock-hard from the memory of her flush this morning at breakfast—eyes tracking water down my chest as I rose from the pool, that telltale hitch in her breath she tried to hide.

"All contestants to the main deck immediately! Challenge time!"

Perfect fucking timing. Nothing burns off this restless, possessive energy like a challenge.

By the time I hit the main deck, Lyla is already there. Skin still carrying that faint flush from breakfast, white bikini top cupping her breasts perfectly, denim shorts showcasing her ass in a way that makes me clench my jaw. She must sense me approaching, because then her whole body tenses—shoulders squaring, chin lifting like armor.

She's still processing. Still fighting what we both feel.

The other female contestants flank her like bodyguards, but I catch the quick glance she steals—eyes locking on mine for half a heartbeat before darting away.

"Good morning, couples!" Miranda sweeps in wearing a red dress that barely qualifies as clothing. "I hope you're all feeling...physical today."

Something about her tone sets my instincts on edge. Cameras repositioned—more of them, tighter angles. Crew buzzing harder than usual. This isn't another trust exercise.

"Ladies," she purrs, "today you get to sit back and watch the men compete for your attention. Literally."

My pulse kicks up. Beside me, Damon straightens—interested, calculating. I see his gaze flick toward Lyla. I clench my hands into fists.

"Gentlemen, you'll be participating in a tournament. Single elimination, bracket style. Seven men, three rounds, one winner."

A tournament. Physical. Raw. I coil with anticipation.

"You'll be competing in a pushing battle." She gestures as PAs wheel out a bracket board. "Three-minute matches where the men will compete in a pit to push each other out. No strikes or no intentional injury are allowed— This is about strength, strategy, and who wants it more."

Who wants it more.

I almost laugh. Less than twelve hours ago, I had Lyla backed against the villa doors, thumb on her lips, telling her I'd rather die than walk away again. Now I get to prove it in the sand.

"The prize," Miranda continues with perfect dramatic timing, "is a private helicopter tour later today. Just the winner and his chosen companion will enjoy a secluded beach, gourmet picnic, and champagne... Complete privacy, with the exception of remote cameras, naturally."

Secluded beach. No producers. Only a few mounted cameras.

I can work with that.

My blood heats. A few stolen hours alone with Lyla—no group chatter, no Damon hovering, no eyes except that one lens. Enough time to come clean about everything. Enough time to make her remember exactly what she's trying to deny.

I find her in the crowd. Her eyes widen as understanding seems to dawn— She knows exactly what I'm about to do.

The producers think they're manufacturing drama. They just handed me the perfect weapon.

Fuck yes!

"Beach in fifteen minutes!" Miranda chirps. "Gentlemen, might want to stretch."

The group scatters. Damon steps in close, voice low.

"Convenient timing." He sounds almost amused.

I meet his eyes. "Meaning?"

"I know about your little heart-to-heart with Lyla during our date. I'm not an idiot. Almost feels like the universe is throwing you a bone." He nods toward the sand circle. "That intense conversation you just had with Lyla. Now this."

I turn to face him square. "Or maybe it's giving me the chance to back up what I said."

"And if you lose?"

In the Corps, that word doesn't exist, isn't an option.

"I won't."

His smile is thin, sharp. "Careful, Scott. Confidence isn't a strategy."

I step into his space just enough to be intimidating. "I made her a promise. This is me keeping it."

"Fighting for someone isn't the same as fighting over them."

I brush past him, my shoulder clipping his lightly. "Good thing I can do both."

The beach setup is simple but brutal. A fifteen-foot circle etched in sand, rope boundary, cameras circling like vultures. The morning sun climbs toward noon; heat is already thick, pressing.

I strip off my shirt. Lyla tries not to look and fails spectacularly. Her gaze drags down my chest, slow, hungry, before she seems to catch herself, notice I'm staring back, and her cheeks bloom red.

That's right, little one. Look at what you're trying to deny.

"Ball draws. Whoever's colored ball matches with another person, is assigned as their opponent. Whoever draws a white ball, will sit out of the challenge." a producer calls.

I match with Sean—a perfect warm-up. Damon draws Nick. Zayne gets Trevor. Bradley is the odd man out and he stands beside the female contestants.

"First match: Scott versus Sean!" Miranda announces.

Sean bounces into the circle, all cocky jitters and misplaced swagger. Behind him, Lyla grips Valerie's arm—knuckles white, eyes wide.

Is she worried about me? The thought sends a dark, possessive thrill straight through my veins. Good. Let her watch what happens when someone threatens what's mine.

"Ready to get your ass kicked?" Sean taunts, circling with a grin that's all bravado.

Fuck around and find out, bozo.

I stay silent. In Afghanistan, the loudest guy was usually the first to die.

The whistle shrieks.

He charges—straight line, all power, predictable as hell. I wait until the last second, feet planted, then pivot hard. His momentum carries him past; I clamp an arm around his waist and redirect, using his own force to spin him off-balance. He staggers, catches himself, and spins back with surprising quickness.

"Lucky move," he growls, wiping sand from his cheek.

We lock up properly this time—chest to chest, forearms braced. His strength is real—gym built, determined. For a second, he gains leverage, shoving me back toward the rope, breath hot against my neck.

Then I catch Lyla leaning forward, lips parted, eyes locked on me like the rest of the world has vanished. Her chest rises and falls faster than it should, thighs press together under those denim shorts.

That's all I need.

I drop my center low, break his grip with a sharp twist, and explode into a hip throw. The impact sends sand spraying in a wide arc; he hits hard on his back with a grunt that echoes. Before he can scramble up, I clamp his arm, roll my weight, and drag him across the line in one controlled, relentless pull.

"Winner: Scott! Fifty-three seconds!"

The crowd erupts—cheers, whistles, a few gasps. I rise, chest heaving, sand clinging to my sweat-slick skin. Lyla still stares, cheeks flushed, fingers digging into Valerie's arm like she's anchoring herself. Her lips part on a silent breath.

I don't smile. I just hold her gaze for one long second—letting her sink into my stare.

The other matches blur past in quick cuts. Zayne overpowers Trevor with raw, working-man force—grunts and thuds—until Trevor taps out fast. But Damon? Damon is different. He moves like water. Patient, precise, every motion economical. When Nick charges, Damon sidesteps, catches him mid-stride, and drops him with a clean, textbook takedown. Nothing about this shows energy wasted, much less showboating. Only control.

Our eyes meet across the churned sand. No words need to be said for both of us to know what happens next.

"Semifinals! Zayne, Damon, and Scott will compete for the finals. The last two left standing will advance!"

Moments after the three of us take our positions in the sand, the whistle blows again.

Immediately, chaos erupts. Zayne goes straight for Damon. It's a smart move. Target the biggest threat first.

They grapple near the center, Zayne's raw power against Damon's slippery patience.

I stay back, watching angles, breathing steady, and preserving what energy I have left.

When Zayne overextends minutes later, I strike.

Closing in fast, I drop low, and hook Zayne's legs from the side while Damon keeps him pinned. Together we shove him over the rope.

"Final round!" Miranda's voice carries over the crowd. "Scott versus Damon!"

Now it's just us.

Damon and I circle once—slow, measuring. The sand is hot under my feet, sun beating down on bare skin. Sweat stings my eyes. Every muscle in my body coils, ready.

When the whistle blows, Damon lunges first. Feigning left, he moves right. I'm quick to block, counter, and lock forearms with him. We strain chest to chest. Sand kicking up with every shift of weight.

He's good. Better than good. He slips a choke attempt; I break it with an elbow, turn in, and drive my shoulder into his ribs.

He grunts but doesn't fold.

We break apart for a heartbeat before locking again. This time harder, faster, desperate. His arm snakes around my neck, pressure building fast.

Layla's sharp gasp cuts through the noise, and something primal ignites within me.

No. Not while she's watching. Not after every promise I made.

Dropping my hips, I move my body upward, and break the hold. I then turn inside his guard. We're chest to chest again. He looks just as tired as I feel. We're both shaking with exhaustion, sand caked to sweat.

"She's not yours," I growl, low enough that only he hears.

"Not yours either," he rasps back. "Not anymore."

"Fuck you."

I hook his leg, lift with everything I have left, and slam him down. The impact rattles through us both. Sand explodes outward as he hits the ground hard. I'm quick to recover, clamp his shoulders, and shove him across the boundary with one final, relentless surge.

His heel crosses the rope, and that's all I need.

"Winner: Scott Bennett!"

I drop to my knees in the sand, chest heaving, ears ringing. The crowd roars, but all I hear is my pulse.

When I look up, Lyla's at the circle's edge, her eyes wide, lips parted. Something between fear and raw hunger flickers across her face.

I stand slowly, walking toward her. Tower over her as she looks up at me, breath shallow.

"I told you I'd fight for us."

She opens her mouth, then closes it. She simply stares as though she's seeing me for the first time.

"Today," I say quietly, just for her. "You and me."

It's not a question.

Before she can answer, Damon appears. Sand is embedded deep in his hair. A bruise is already blooming on his forearm.

"Good fight," he says to me, voice even as he extends his hand. After I accept, his gaze turns to Lyla. "Can we talk?"

The second Lyla nods, she and Damon walk down to the shoreline. As they go, she glances back once. In that glance, I see everything—the war with herself; what she thinks she wants versus what she knows she needs.

Our date can't come fast enough.

Lyla

My hands are shaking so hard I have to clasp them behind my back.

Scott and Damon circle each other in the pit, chests heaving, sand plastered to sweat. The producers have created a gladiator farce, and now the final round is exactly what everyone secretly wanted: two men fighting like their lives depend on who gets to keep me.

This is horrible, but I can't stop watching.

Scott moves like he was born for this—controlled violence, eyes scanning for the opening that ends it. Every roll of muscle under his skin reminds me how those same shoulders caged me against the villa wall two nights ago, how his grip turned gentle the second I whimpered his name.

Damon counters with heart and fury, refusing to fold even when he's clearly spent. There's something almost noble in it, something that should make me feel safe.

Instead, it just makes the ache between my legs sharper.

They crash together—grunts, flesh slapping flesh, the wet smack of sweat. Scott absorbs Damon's charge, plants, and twists. For a moment, they stalemate.

Then Damon hooks an arm around Scott's throat.

The choke sinks in deep. Scott's face flushes dark, veins standing out in his neck. He doesn't panic. But he can't breathe.

"No," I whisper, the word ripping out before I can stop it.

My vision narrows to Scott's struggling form. The thought of him going limp—of losing him again, even for a stupid game—hits like a hole punching through my chest.

But then Scott's elbow drives back, hard and deliberate. The impact breaks Damon's hold, and they separate, both staggering.

They're chest to chest now, both shaking, sweat carving clean tracks through the sand on their skin. I can't hear every word over the crowd and the surf, but Scott's low growl cuts through anyway.

"She's not yours."

Whatever Damon snarls back seems to light a fuse in Scott.

"Fuck you."

Scott moves—fast, brutal. He hooks Damon's leg, lifts, and drives him down. The thud of impact rolls through the sand and into my chest. Damon's breath explodes out of him; Scott doesn't let up. Then with one final, relentless shove, Damon's heel drags across the rope boundary.

It's over.

The crowd erupts around me. But the noise fades to a dull roar in my ears. All I see is Scott standing alone in the center of the pit, chest heaving, blood trickling from his lip, and sand streaking across every carved inch of him like war paint.

His eyes lock on mine.

There's no smile, no triumphant gloat. Just raw, unfiltered possession. *You're mine.*

The words aren't spoken, but I feel them in my bones.

I should be furious. This is barbaric. Objectifying. Everything I told myself I'd never let myself want again. Instead, I'm burning, rooted in place, pulse throbbing where it has no business throbbing. Heat surges low and insistent. My nipples pebble against the thin fabric of my bikini top.

"Damn, girl," Kylie mutters beside me, elbow nudging my ribs. "Your face is screaming *take me right here.*"

I swallow hard. My mouth is dry while the rest of me is anything but.

Scott wipes the blood from his lip with the back of his hand. His eyes never leave mine. Then he starts walking toward me like no one else exists.

I'm so screwed.

Miranda's voice slices through the chaos. "Winner: Scott Bennett!"

The crowd surges, cheering and pressing in, but Scott moves through them like smoke. He walks straight for me, still breathing hard, sand and sweat streaking his torso in filthy, mesmerizing patterns. Each deliberate step eats the distance between us, purposeful, predatory.

My heart hammers against my ribs as he stops inches away. This close, I can see the exhaustion and relief in his eyes, smell the heady mix of exertion and raw male musk rolling off his skin. It's intoxicating. Overwhelming.

"Today," he says, voice gravel-rough from the fight, loud enough for every contestant, every camera, every microphone to catch. "Helicopter tour. You and me."

It's not a question. The absolute certainty in his tone sends a sharp, involuntary clench low in my belly, heat pooling between my thighs despite everything.

Before I can scrape together words, Damon steps up to my elbow. Sand dusts his hair; a fresh bruise is forming along his forearm. His composure is still mostly intact, but there's a tighness around his eyes that wasn't there before.

"Good fight," he tells Scott. The words are clipped. Then his gaze shifts to me, softer but no less intense. "Lyla, can we talk?"

The air between the two men crackles—pure testosterone, barely leashed. Scott's jaw ticks once, hard; his stance goes rigid like he's physically holding himself back from dragging Damon into the pit and finishing what the rope stopped.

I nod, throat tight, and follow Damon toward the shoreline. Every step feels weighted. I don't need to look to know Scott's eyes are burning holes into my back—possessive, patient, promising.

"He's confident," Damon says once the crowd noise fades behind us. "Almost like he already knows the outcome."

"Nobody's won anything."

He stops, turning to face me fully. His eyes are steady, assessing. "Maybe not yet. But that man just fought through three guys for you, and the way you looked at him in that pit... You weren't exactly rooting for the underdog."

Heat surges into my cheeks, instant and guilty. "I didn't—"

"Lyla." His voice is gentle, but there's an edge of knowing underneath. "I'm not blind. There's history between you two that runs deeper than anything we've just started here. And right now, your body is screaming louder than your head."

I wrap my arms around myself as if that could shield me from the truth. "It's complicated."

"I know." He steps closer. "But here's what I see: a woman who's terrified to admit what she wants because it scares her. A woman who's drawn to the chaos."

"That's not—" I start, but the denial dies on my tongue. Because part of me hears the truth in it, even if it's only half the picture.

"I'm not giving up," he says, his tone shifting to calm determination. Certainty. "He may have won the challenge, but he hasn't won you. Real relationships aren't built on who can slam the other guy hardest. They're built on showing up every day, without needing to prove something."

I glance back toward the crowd of contestants and producers. Scott is exactly where we left him—pacing like a caged panther, eyes locked on us, every muscle coiled with barely leashed restraint.

Damon follows my gaze. A small, wry smile touches his mouth. "You're still here talking to me. He's over there, yet you chose to walk away with me. That tells me something."

I swallow hard. "I should get back."

"While you're on that helicopter..." He holds my eyes, unflinching. "Ask yourself one thing. Does he see you as a partner or as a prize to be fought for and claimed? Because from where I'm standing, he's trying to win you back the same way he won today: through sheer, unrelenting force."

The words sink deep, sharp and undeniable.

As we walk back, Scott's stare never leaves us. It prickles across my skin: hot, heavy, promising.

Partner or prize?

The question burrows in my mind and refuses to let go.

Chapter Twelve

Lyla

The helicopter waits on the beach an hour later like a promise and a threat, rotors already slicing the humid air. Cameras circle us, greedy for every loaded glance, every careful touch as Scott helps me climb inside. I'm hyperaware of the lenses trained on us, but that doesn't stop the traitorous urge to press closer to him. To cling like he's the only thing left.

Behind us, the other contestants have gathered to watch us leave. Damon stands apart, arms crossed, expression carefully blank. Our eyes meet for a moment. He gives one slow nod.

Scott's hand settles at my lower back. Warm, possessive, steady through the thin fabric of my dress. "Ready?"

I'm angry, yet there's something deeper I feel. Something that makes me want more. Something I'm too terrified to acknowledge, which only confuses me further. How can someone resent and want a person at the same time? So no. I'm not ready to be alone with him. Not like this.

Avoiding this would be easier than facing it head-on.

"Let's go," a producer yells over the rotors to the pilot.

We lift off the ground, and the villa shrinks below us. Scott sits close enough that our thighs touch, his heat seeping through my sundress. Neither of us speaks as the Caribbean unrolls beneath us—crystalline water, scattered islands, paradise that feels more and more like purgatory the longer this show stretches on.

The pilot's presence and the tiny cameras affixed to the corners of the cabin, make the silence suffocating. Every breath feels watched. Every accidental brush of Scott's leg against mine has my senses going into overload.

Minutes that feel more like hours later, an island materializes below. A perfect crescent of white sand edged by dense jungle, looking utterly isolated. No doubt cameras lurk in every palm tree and crevice anyway.

As we descend, I spot the setup: an elegant pavilion on the beach, gauze curtains already snapping in a rising wind, a table for two laid with linens and crystal that look ready to blow away.

Dark clouds mass on the horizon, boiling forward faster than seems possible. The sky behind us is still bright blue while ahead it's turning iron-gray.

"Storm's comin'," the pilot says as the skids kiss sand. "Movin' quicker than forecasted. Producers want me to tell you we'll monitor from the mainland, but if this weather hits directly, head for the bungalow. You should be fine."

I brush off the warning. Good to know we don't have to wait outside for help if a storm does come.

Scott unbuckles quickly and turns to face me. His eyes meet mine—quiet, unreadable, but carrying the same weight they've held since the challenge.

The pilot points through the palms. "Bungalow's that way if you need it." He points to the small building. "Fully stocked, reinforced for hurricanes. You should have power since the place runs on a generator."

Then he's gone, rotors fading into the gray sky.

Even though we're the only ones on this island, my shoulders stay tight. The setup allows us just enough emptiness to drop our guards, to coax out whatever emotions or physical actions the producers want for the edit. I feel like doing the exact opposite.

Scott pulls a chair out for me with automatic courtesy, then takes the seat across from me. The elaborate spread—champagne chilling, fruit glistening, candles already guttering—looks ridiculous against the darkening sky.

"Hungry?" Scott asks, but his gaze stays on the approaching clouds, not the elaborate spread already trembling under the rising wind.

I chew slowly on a finger sandwich and stare out into the gray, almost black, sky. The turquoise ocean. Anywhere but at him. My pulse picks up at the growing seconds that tick by.

The first gust whips my hair across my face. The gauze curtains on the pavilion snap like flags in surrender.

What could possibly have been his motive for winning? Better yet, his reason for even being here? I know he's said he came for me, but that could mean anything.

If he wanted the latter, he would have done it already.

True, but for all I know he could be playing the long game.

What is he hoping to get out of this entire experience? Was the grass not as green on the other side as he thought it was?

This line of thinking is getting dangerous.

I'd rather not be here, but the thought of going back to the villa isn't all that enticing, either. I'm stuck. And something tells me, with this large, dark and looming cloud coming, the next couple of minutes are going to dictate what happens next.

"So much for the romantic dinner," I mutter, gesturing at the table as small drops of rain begin to pelt the linens. The candles flicker and die one by one. Seeing them extinguish feels predictable.

There's also the question of why he's on this show in the first place. A question, since he showed up on the dock, I've chosen to ignore. But the more time has gone on, the more that questions keeps invading my thoughts. A part of me wants to at least hear the excuse and be done with it. Maybe then he'd disappear into the depths of the past. But that other part, the part that's fearful of what he might say, is just as loud.

It'd be up to me whether or not to believe his "truth."

"Congrats," I say, my voice thick with sarcasm. "Now that you have me here, what's your grand plan?"

Scott's jaw tightens. Leaning forward, his eyes lock on mine. "How else could I get you to talk to me?"

"About what exactly? I have nothing to say, so nothing needs to be said."

He rests his elbows on the table, leaning impossibly closer. "It's a giant fucking elephant in the room with us. It needs to be said."

"And what would that be? *Your* shitty choices?" I throw his words right back at him. "You've made your bed. Why can't you just lie in it like I have?"

"Because there's more to the story than you know. And you should know."

"Oh, so that's why you're here. I'm unfinished business for you," I say with fake and sarcastic enthusiasm. Damon's words echo in my head. *Does he see you as a partner...or a prize?*

Scott shakes his head as if in annoyance.

I continue. "You're only here because you want to twist some shitty-ass narrative where you're the victim in your decision-making. Not that you found some greener grass somewhere and was too much of a coward to say it was over to my face."

At first, he doesn't say anything, his head down. Then he looks back up at me as if he's thought of something. "You seem rather confident about my motives when you don't even know the reasoning behind them."

I lean back in my chair, arms crossed. "I don't have to assume. I was a casualty of your motives."

"So you're perfectly content with hating me, even when you don't have the whole story?" He arches a brow, staring at me skeptically.

"What other part of this story is there to tell? You left for yourself. End of story."

Before he can argue back, the wind whips the gauze curtains sideways, and the sky opens.

All at once, rain comes down hard and horizontal in seconds, soaking us instantly.

Scott is immediately on his feet. "We need to get to shelter. Now."

He eats the distance between us, reaching for my hand. I push it away. "I'm not going anywhere with you."

"So you'd rather die in this storm."

I scoff. "Please, I'm not going to die. Don't be so dramatic."

"Lyla, don't do this."

"Do what? I'm perfectly fine where I am."

In all honesty, I'm not. But anywhere is better than near him.

I look off into the horizon, lifting my chin in defiance.

"Yeah? Well, I'm not fine with it."

Before I can protest, he has me over his shoulder, walking away from the table.

I kick and scream, hitting his broad, muscled back with my fists. "Put me down, you rat bastard."

Ignoring me, he makes his way to the small bungalow. My sundress clings like a second skin. My hair is soaked and sticking to my neck, falling into my face.

All I can see in front of me is the roaring storm and the heels of his feet on the sand below.

"Stop squirming."

"Fuck you," I scream, balking in anger.

When we reach the shelter, he opens a sliding door and steps inside. Sand is replaced with white-tiled floor.

The storm is muffled once he closes the door behind him. I feel his hands on my feet as he takes my shoes off.

"Can you put me down now?"

"Are you going to behave?"

"I'm not a child."

"Says the woman who insisted on staying out in a tropical storm just out of spite."

I hesitate, mostly out of embarrassment. "Fine."

"Good girl." He sets me gently on my feet.

The shelter is small but solid. An open-concept space with only a translucent ivory curtain dividing a king bed at the far wall from the rest of the space. A kitchen with bare-bones essentials is to our immediate left. A living room rests between the two. The more I look around, the more I realize it's more a modern bungalow than an emergency shelter. If I wasn't so angry, and he wasn't standing next to me, I could admire this more.

Scott walks farther into the space and into the small living room before taking off his rain-soaked shirt with a wet slap and sitting on one of the chairs.

I gape at him. Every move he makes, every muscle that shifts under his tanned skin, is something I can't look away from. I unconsciously bite my lip.

No. Resist, Lyla. Resist.

I gasp when the lights begin to flicker. I tense as they strobe once. Twice. Then hold.

"D-do you think we'll lose power?" I stammer.

He glances at the large windows, where wind is already shoving chairs across the deck. "At this point, I don't think it's a question of if we lose power. It might be when. The pilot said this place runs on a generator. At this rate, I'm wondering if it might fail on us."

"Fail? You mean, we could lose power?"

"Likely, but anything's possible."

An impossible fantasy of real privacy—of no eyes and ears—suddenly doesn't seem so crazy. But never did it involve him. Didn't involve being in this tiny space in a convenient tropical storm where we could very much be stuck in the dark and lose complete contact with the outside world. At least for however long it lasts.

I slowly walk farther into the room when he scans me up and down. Heat crawls up my face.

"You're shivering," he says softly.

He's right, but it's not just from the cold.

"I'll go find some candles, just in case." I fumble into the kitchen and through half-filled drawers, desperate for anything to do other than stare at the all-consuming, half-naked man sitting just behind me.

The growing storm I see from the large window above the sink mirrors the one inside me as I gather different kinds and types of candles along with a box of matches. Violent, destructive, and perhaps inevitable.

When I walk back into the living room, I'm met with him offering a glass of wine he'd found. An array of rations are splayed across the coffee table in the middle. "Not quite like the five-star spread that was out there, but..."

I accept the glass, handing him the candles and matches in exchange. "It's fine." The sight is actually impressive.

"Come sit." He gestures for me to sit on the couch with him.

As if on cue, the lights flicker again—once, twice—then die completely. Light from the afternoon sky is the only thing that keeps the place from being pitch black.

I panic. "Oh, god. Scott?"

"It's okay," he assures.

I can't help but sigh in relief as he takes a gentle but firm hold of my hand and guides me as to the couch.

"Thank you." I feel with my hand for the cushion before sitting down.

Probably sensing I was okay, he lets go of my arm. He sits down beside me.

He stands back up, looking around the living space. He then goes into the kitchen, coming back a few minutes later with a handful, plus matches and emergency supplies.

"How can you see with such dim lighting?"

I hear him chuckle. "Years and years of practice."

When he sits back down again, he lights a match. A bright tiny flame appears in front of me. I capture a glimpse of Scott's face as he begins to light each candle I'd found before setting them down on the table beside the food.

My eyes adjust slowly to the candle glow. I'm relieved to be able to see again. Outside, the storm howls as though in victory.

I'm quick to notice Scott's pants are just as rain soaked as his shirt, clinging low on his hips, water trailing slow paths down the ridges of his abs and into the parts beneath the fabric. Every muscle is etched sharp in the dimming light.

Scott is looking around the space like I am when he stands up with one of the taller candles in hand, walks over to a corner of the space, and holds the candle up to a camera I didn't realize was there.

Damn, they hide those things better than I thought.

As if satisfied, he moves on to the next one in his line of sight. Then the next.

"What are you doing?" I can't help but feel hope surge through me.

"Confirming something." When he reaches the camera that captures the threshold of the bedroom, he smiles. "Exactly what I thought. Cameras are down."

I almost don't believe his words. "You're sure?"

He nods as he retreats to the couch. "No recording red light. No hum. I don't even think they have a surge protector. Safe to say the storm shot their wiring to death."

I glance down at the portable mic clipped to me, frowning. "But they can still hear us."

When I look back at him, he seems to be contemplating something, as if an opportunity has landed in his lap.

"What is it?" I ask.

He doesn't say anything. Instead, he reaches behind him, yanking his own mic off, and turns it off.

I look at him with wide eyes. "What are you—"

He shushes me with a finger to his lips, then points to my mic, gesturing for me to give it to him.

I hesitate. In part, because I know it's a bad idea. But at the same time...

I peel the mic from my body and place it in his palm. He's quick to switch it off and set both our mics on the table like discarded restraints.

"Won't they try to contact us and try to get to us if they don't know what's going on?"

"If this storm is as big as it is, chances are they're having issues over at the villa, too. We'll have at least a couple of hours to ourselves."

Awkward silence falls between us. It's palpable.

Scott remains sitting, his gaze locked onto mine. Candlelight carves shadows across his bare chest. Water still beads down from his hair and onto his skin. I should look away, but I can't. Can't reject what he's silently asking. He, and this situation, make it impossible.

He looks at me like he's bracing for something worse than the hurricane outside.

"You deserve to at least have closure."

I shake my head. What would be the point? "It was so—"

"Don't tell me knowing why doesn't matter to you, because I know it does. You can't lie to me, little one. You, and this, have everything to do with why I'm on this show."

I shrug, trying to feign indifference. "So what? You're just going to say it regardless of how I feel?"

"I'm going to say it because I *know* how you feel."

I hesitate. "I don't—"

"I never left because I stopped wanting you," he starts anyway. "I left because I didn't want to lose you. Creating distance was the only way I knew you'd be protected, be able to live your life peacefully."

I tilt my head in confusion from his riddle of an explanation. "You left to not lose me? Creating distance to protect me? That doesn't make any sense."

He sighs. "I didn't talk much about him to you back then because I didn't want to put you in the middle of our beef or to worry about me."

"Him? I don't understand—"

"It was Vincent."

"Vincent? Like your father?"

He nods.

I vaguely remember back then Scott mentioning him. But those times were few and far between—and usually he was venting to me in anger and frustration. The very few times I'd met the man, he was rather condescending, but Scott ran enough interference to make our few interactions civil.

"What about him?"

"He was the reason I had to leave."

Silence lands heavy after his words as I process what he just said.

Did I... Did I hear that right?

He leans closer, meeting my eyes. His eyes are filled with pain, raw, unguarded, like something inside him just cracked wide open.

The candle flames waver between us.

"During the spring break before I left, he'd found out about us. Exactly how he did? I have no idea. I just know that when we got back from that trip, he told me to break if off with you and that I had until graduation to, as he put it, *find a more suitable match*."

I'm taken aback with shock and disgust, but I let him continue.

"As you probably had guessed the few times you two met, he cared very much about what high society thought. And his thoughts when you weren't around often bled into my love life. Into how he felt about you and your family."

"What an asshole. I knew he was a piece of work, but that's awful."

Scott gives a small grin of amusement. "Exactly what I said to his face when he demanded I take another girl out to dinner on your birthday instead of you because he wanted to do business with her family's company. I refused."

I can't help but beam at him for protecting me like that. When the world seemed absolute bliss with him, it was chaos, unbeknownst to me. And even then, even when he was given the easy way out, he chose me anyway.

He then sobers. "By the time graduation rolled around, and he found out you and I were still dating, he went crazy. Blazing mad that night. He then gave me an ultimatum. Dump you right there and then, or you and your family would, as he said, *suffer and blame me for it.*"

"Suffer? How?"

He hesitates as though suddenly uncomfortable. "Financially, socially. He'd cripple you to the point of bankruptcy and utter ruin. Blacklist your parents from ever working in their fields again. Knowing the money and connections he had, I couldn't take the chance that he was bluffing. Not that time."

I gasp in horror. "What father would do that to his son?"

"That was Vincent Bennett. Always used to getting what he wanted, and was willing to play dirty to get it." Scott pauses. "I didn't want to give in, but I didn't want to lose you either. But I knew that if I didn't do as he said, you'd suffer. I was scared you'd blame me over time."

I shake my head profusely.

He looks at me with sad eyes. "You would have eventually, Lyla, because even your college scholarship was on the table."

All I can do is listen and feel tears sting my eyes. "So you left."

Tears fill his eyes, too.

The room tilts. I press a hand to my chest. The more I piece together, the more everything starts to make sense. Why he vanished as if into thin air, why I never heard of or from him ever again. I'd spent ten years wondering what happened. And just as long convincing myself

I wasn't worth an explanation and would have been better off to have cried, hurt, and bled alone.

"W-where did you go? Where have you been after all this time?"

"I joined the Marines."

"You what? How long?"

"Ten years. Spent about six months after I left home in boot camp and SOI training. Then deployments for the next one hundred and fourteen months."

I sit there in disbelief. You can't make this shit up. "Why didn't you send me any letters? Call me?"

He takes both my hands in his. "I couldn't be sure what my father would do if he found out I'd made contact with you."

"Then...why are you here if you're worried about my safety like this?"

His mouth forms a genuine smile. "He'd died six months ago. I've been back in Dallas for four months."

I'm shocked even further. "He died?"

He nods. "I made arrangements to get back to Dallas the same day I found out. Got out two months later. Imagine my surprise when I found out I'd inherited everything." He shakes his head as though still in disbelief by that piece of information.

"So you'd been in Texas for four months and didn't think to at least call?

"Until I got a call about the show, I was still trying to figure out how to approach you without a door slamming in my face, much less you blocking my number if I called."

I stand up, anger flaring. "You could spend ten years of your life as a Marine, but you couldn't find the courage to at least call me for four months once you knew he was dead?"

He crosses his arms. "I didn't think it'd be exactly romantic for our first time in ten years seeing each other to be over FaceTime."

"Everything I've done, from the moment I left, was to get back to you." His voice is low, rough. "You think I wanted to do that? You think I wanted to leave you for ten years just to reunite with you on some fucking reality show?"

"Regardless, you chose the outcome of our relationship for me." Even as I ache to touch him, this fact is something I can't deny.

"There were so many times I wanted to come back, consequences be damned. But I knew I couldn't. If it's any consolation, I'd found ways over the years to at least know what you were up to. I was so proud of you when you graduated college and started Clark Events. The boys even made fun of me for throwing a small party. And when I got back into Dallas, I did what I could to make sure you were taken care of." His eyes meet mine—raw, open. "But then I also realized that you'd built a life. A business. Friends. I didn't want you thinking I just wanted to drag the past back in and ruin everything."

"You spied on me?" The words taste bitter. "That's sick."

His expression turns blank. Clearly, he hadn't thought through telling me that fact.

"I didn't do it for any kind of perversion. I did it because it was never over for me. And as far as I'm concerned, it still isn't."

Tears burn behind my eyes. Not from anger this time, but from the sheer weight of everything he's telling me, everything he's carried alone for my sake.

I open my mouth, but nothing comes out at first. Then, small and broken, I blurt out the words I never thought I'd get to tell him as I place a hand on my stomach.

"I was pregnant."

Scott goes stone still at my words.

"I'd found out three weeks after you left. I was terrified. Stupidly hopeful that you'd come back and we could be a family. But still terrified. I was young and desperate for your disappearance to make sense. A baby felt like proof that what we had was real, that you didn't just disappear because you got bored of me and were too spineless to tell me it was over."

He makes a sound—half pain, half disbelief. His hand lifts like he wants to touch me, then drops it.

I continue. "I miscarried at twenty weeks. I was alone. I thought if I could make it to the hospital, I could save it. Save our baby." More tears fall from my eyes. "But when I got there, it was too late. No one knew. Not even my parents."

Scott's eyes are glassy. His throat works hard. When he speaks, his voice is wrecked. "Our baby?"

All I can manage is a nod.

He closes the distance in one step, pulling me against him in a warm, tight embrace.

I don't hug him back right away. But I don't pull away either. My tears become two waterfalls against his chest.

"I'm so sorry," he rasps into my hair. "I didn't know. I swear I didn't know."

He's quiet for a long moment as he holds me tightly in one hand, while rubbing my back with the other.

He then lifts his hand from my back and cups my face. His thumb brushes away my tears.

"Tell me," he says, voice wrecked. "Please, tell me about our baby."

The words crack something open inside me.

"The doctor was kind after it was over. Said it wasn't my fault. Let me hold him before they took him away."

Scott's thumb stills against my cheek. His expression turns even more crushed.

"Him?"

I try to smile through the fresh tears forming and blurring my vision. "I wanted to name him Michael, after your middle name. I kept thinking"—my voice breaks—"what if the stress of losing you did it? What if I carried all that grief and shame and it poisoned him?"

"No." The word is fierce, almost violent. He shakes his head, both his hands now frame my face. "Don't do that to yourself. None of it was your fault. It was mine."

I shake my head. "I should've—"

"Stop." His voice cracks on the word. "It's mine. For leaving. For not being there. For every single day you carried him alone."

I swallow hard. The candlelight flickers across his face, catching the sheen in his eyes.

"He would've been perfect." His voice is hoarse. "Just like his mother."

"Don't." I turn my gaze away. "Don't romanticize me. I'm not perfect. I'm broken. I spent ten years hating you."

His forehead rests against mine. Our breaths mingle—ragged, uneven. The storm shrieks louder outside, but in here, the only sound is our hearts trying to find the same rhythm again.

He wraps his arms around me. Arms lock around my back, pulling me impossibly closer. For a long moment, we continue to just breathe, tasting of salt, rain, and grief.

Then his mouth finds mine.

The kiss isn't careful. It isn't possessive. It's pure, aching need. Like ten years of hunger and regret are compressed into this one all-consuming kiss. I taste the salt of our tears and the faint edge of wine still on his breath.

One of his hands fists in my hair, tilting my head back.

I rest my arms around his torso.

When his mouth travels down my jaw and his teeth graze the pulse at my throat, a moan rips out of me that's quickly swallowed by thunder.

"Scott—" I breathe.

"Tell me to stop," he rasps against my skin. His lips brush the spot he just bit. "Say the word, and I'll stop."

I can't.

I don't want to.

"Don't," I whisper, fingers now having traveled to his shoulder, digging into his skin. "Please don't stop."

His growl hits low against my throat—rough, frayed, like he's been holding himself together too long and the thread has finally snapped.

One hand slides down my back, bunching the soaked sundress until the hem clears my thighs, and cool air hits skin that's been burning since he popped back into my life. The other hand cups my jaw, thumb dragging through the mess of rain and tears he still can't wipe away. Then he lifts me.

My legs lock around his waist like they never forgot the shape of him.

He carries me three steps to the bed. The mattress dips under our weight. Scott settles above and surrounding me—solid heat, wet skin, rainwater dripping from his hair onto my collarbone, mixing with the salt already there.

For one long moment, we just breathe. He holds me tight against his chest. He leans his forehead to mine. I can feel his heart slamming against my ribs like it's trying to reach mine through bone and ten years of silence.

"I need to see you," he rasps, voice cracked open. "All of you. Please."

That *please* slices me open wider than any knife ever could.

I nod—shaking, tears still leaking—and lift my arms. His thumbs hook under the thin straps of my sundress—slow, reverent, like he's afraid the fabric might dissolve if he moves too fast. Rainwater has turned it nearly transparent; every inch of me is already on display, but he wants the last veil gone.

The dress slides up, over my head, and lands somewhere behind us with a wet slap. My bra and panties cling uselessly, translucent from rain. His fingers tremble at the edges as he unhooks the bra, slides the straps down my arms, and lets it fall. My skin is all goose bumped and flushed. My nipples are tight from cold and want and the way his eyes devour me like he's starving.

"Jesus, Lyla." His voice is gravel. He sits back on his heels between my thighs, palms skating up my sides, thumbs brushing the undersides of my breasts. "You're more beautiful than I remembered. And I remembered every fucking detail."

I swallow hard. "You had ten years to forget."

"Never." He leans down, mouth hovering over one nipple, breath hot. "Every deployment. Every night I couldn't sleep. It was always your face. Your laugh. The way you tasted." His tongue flicks out—once, testing the nub. Then he sucks hard, drawing a gasp from me that echoes in the room.

My fingers dig into his wet hair. "Scott—"

He switches to the other side, delivers the same rough worship, same growl vibrating through me. One hand slides down, cupping me through soaked panties. Not pushing yet. Just holding. Feeling how drenched I am for him.

"How many others?" The question slips out before I can stop it—quiet, cracked. I hate that it still matters.

He freezes. Lifts his head. Eyes dark, pained. "A handful. None lasted longer than a night or two." His thumb hovers over the cotton covering my clit. "None of them were you. I'd close my eyes and picture you instead of them. Every time."

My throat burns. "I tried, too. A few times. Always ended with me crying in the shower afterward, wishing it was you touching me." I arch into his hand, begging him to circle his thumb there. "It never stopped hurting."

He exhales like I've punched him. "I'm so fucking sorry I wasn't there when you lost him." His forehead drops to my stomach—right over the place our baby once was. "I should've been holding you. Telling you it wasn't your fault. Begging you to let me stay."

Tears slip hot down my temples. "You can hold me now."

He does. Both arms band around my waist, face pressed to my skin like he's trying to crawl inside me and rewrite history. Then he kisses lower—open-mouthed, desperate—trailing fire down my ribs, over the soft curve of my belly.

When he reaches the edge of my panties, he looks up. Eyes blazing. "Let me make it right. Let me taste you. Let me worship the woman who carried our baby even when I couldn't be there."

My legs fall open wider on instinct. "Yes."

He doesn't hesitate. Hooking the fabric aside, he parts me gently with his fingers, then seals his mouth over me like reclaiming territory he lost a decade ago.

Hungry. Relentless. He circles his tongue over my bundle of nerves in slow, firm strokes while his hands clamp on my hips, holding me exactly where he wants me.

I writhe under the instant, overwhelming pleasure and, at the same time, spread myself wider—too much, too good, too soon. He growls against me, the vibration ripping a whimper from my throat, and tightens his grip. No escape. No mercy. Just his mouth devouring me like he's starving and I'm the only thing that could ever satisfy him.

"I love how you taste," he murmurs between licks, voice muffled against my slick heat. "Love the sounds you make when I do this—" He sucks my clit hard into his mouth.

I bow my back off the bed from the immediate contact, the relentless pressure. Something between a moan and a scream tears from my throat. My fingers twist in his wet hair, pulling him closer even as my thighs shake around his head.

He explores every inch, lapping deep, then shallow, tracing every fold like he's memorizing me again. No part of me escapes his mouth. Pleasure coils tighter, hotter, until I'm right on the edge, hips grinding seamlessly against his face.

Then he pulls back.

"Not yet."

"Please—" The word sobs out of me. "Scott, please, I need—"

"I know what you need, little one." He slides two thick fingers inside me, curling just right against that spot that makes stars burst behind my eyelids. He pumps slowly, watching my face. "You need to come, don't you? Need me to let you fall apart on my tongue?"

I nod frantically, tears slipping free again—not from pain this time, but from how badly I want this. Want him. "Yes. God, yes. Please."

"Such pretty begging." He lowers his head again, lips closing over my clit, and this time he doesn't stop. Fingers thrust in rhythm with his sucking, tongue relentless.

The orgasm hits like a freight train. My whole body locks, thighs clamping around his head as I shatter with a scream—hard, blinding, vision whiting out for a second. I scream his name, hips grinding against his face while he works me through every pulsing aftershock, drawing it out until I'm boneless and trembling.

When I finally come back to myself, he's kissing his way up my body—slow, worshipping trails over my hip, my waist. He pauses at my stomach, lips brushing skin, voice rough. "I'm sorry I wasn't there. For all of it."

He sheds his shorts in one motion. Then he settles between my legs, hard length nudging my entrance—hot, thick, already seeping at the crest. I grind against him on pure instinct, chasing that friction, trying to bury him inside, and we both groan.

This doesn't fix anything.

It doesn't erase ten years. Doesn't rebuild the trust he shattered when he walked away. My heart is still bruised black-and-blue, and one mind-blowing orgasm isn't going to change that. But right now, with his body heat surrounding me and the rain still hammering the windows, I don't want to think about tomorrow's unpredictability.

I just want this.

He leans down. "I'm right here. Right now. Let me have you."

The kiss that follows is messy, hungry, angry—tongues clashing as he swallows the sob caught in my throat. My nails rake down his back, marking him, needing him closer even if it's only for tonight.

He nudges my entrance farther. My whole body trembles. Not just from desire, but from fear, hope, and everything I've buried for a decade.

"Please, Scott."

He pushes in—slow, so slow, stretching me with a delicious burn that blurs pain and pleasure until they're one aching pulse. My breath catches, a broken sound, as he fills me inch by agonizing inch. He's overwhelming, or maybe I'm just too raw after years of emptiness that never quite echoed like this. My nails dig deeper into his back, anchoring me as sensation and emotion twist together in my chest.

When he's buried to the hilt, he stills, forehead pressed to mine, breath ragged against my lips. Beads of sweat form at his temple. "I've missed you," he rasps. "You feel like coming home."

He kisses my lips as he withdraws almost completely, before driving back in one thrust. We both gasp, sharp and shared.

The rhythm builds, relentless. Each thrust is harder, deeper. I wrap him in my legs.

"You take me so perfectly, little one," he growls, voice fraying. "Every inch, like you were waiting for me all this time."

His words spark heat low in my belly; I clench hard around him, and he groans deep in his throat. "You like that? Like being my good girl?"

"Yes," I cry out, the praise unraveling me further. Only need remains when it comes to him.

His hand slips between us, fingers finding that swollen bundle of nerves and circling with agonizing slowness. "Then come for me again. Let me feel you shatter."

Him stroking me deep, his relentless thumb at my core, pushes me further at the edge until a wave of overwhelming pleasure crashes through me in blinding waves. I cry out, body pulsing around him. I clamp hard as I fall over into the fiery pleasure.

He murmurs praise against my ear. "That's it...just like that... Give it all to me."

I tremble through the aftershocks. He doesn't stop. With careful strength, he hooks my legs higher around his waist, lifting my hips to meet his. One hand cups my rear end as he sinks even deeper. Our faces are inches apart with his eyes never leaving mine—dark, desperate, pleading. The new position drags him against every sensitive place, especially hitting my clit, until stars burst behind my closed lids.

"Mine," he growls low, hips snapping with controlled ferocity. Our breaths mingle. Sweat-slick skin slides together as he thrusts in and out of me. "Say it."

His lips brush mine. Heat and need start building in my core again as I tilt my head back. He presses his lips to my exposed throat and collarbone.

I gasp. "Yours. I'm yours."

He thrusts harder, like he's pouring every unspoken apology into my body. Our hands find each other. Fingers lacing tight above my head as he uses the leverage to rock deeper, slower, grinding in circles that make my toes curl.

I pull my head back toward him. "Harder," I beg into his mouth, voice raw. "Please, Scott—I need—"

"Fuck—" His control fractures. His rhythm turns erratic, desperate. Plunging deep, he buries his face in my neck as he pulses hot inside me. He fills me in long, shuddering waves that drag another soft climax from my depths.

We collapse together on the bed, tangled in each other, shaking, our breaths mingling in harsh pants. He stays seated deep, softening slowly, but neither of us moves. My legs stay wrapped around him.

For long moments, we just exist there, chests rising and falling in sync, his head resting against my shoulder, the storm outside a distant rumble compared to the thunder still echoing in my veins. I can feel the faint aftershocks rippling through us both, small flutters where we're joined, his warmth seeping deeper even as he softens. My fingers trace lazy patterns across his back, soothing, memorizing the map of scars and muscles I've missed for so long.

He exhales shakily against my lips. Then shifting his hips, he rocks into me. Enough to stir the sensitive places inside me that haven't quite come down yet. The parts of me that want more. I let out a soft gasp, and my inner walls flutter around him in response.

"With pleasure, little one," he whispers, voice rough and tender at once. He eases into lazy, shallow strokes that keep the afterglow humming between us. Slow glides that coax rather than demand, building heat gradually instead of chasing it.

This time is slower, softer, intimate in a way that tightens my chest. My heart lurches. We stare into each other's eyes, breaths shared, bodies fused like they've remembered every curve. His thumb brushes my cheek, wiping away a stray tear I didn't realize had fallen.

When release finds us again, it's quiet, profound. This moment together, gazes locked, feels like a promise. A fragile brush of souls amid the storm, as though finally breathing after years underwater.

We lie entwined afterward through the night. His arms a warm cage around me, lips brushing my forehead, my temple, the corner of my mouth.

At one point in the night, he buries himself inside me again. "I've got you," he murmurs. "I'm right here."

For now.

A part of me wants to believe him—wants to melt into his warmth and pretend the past decade never happened.

But deep down, the hurt still pulses. The abandonment, the silence, the bone-deep fear he'll vanish again when the storm clears.

Tonight, I'll allow myself this. Curl into his body, let my heartbeat slow to match his, inhale the rain and cedar scent of his skin like it's the only thing keeping me afloat.

Because tomorrow, reality will crash back in. The villa awaits. No doubt another twist in the game looms. There's still so much broken between us, and no amount of tangled limbs, orgasms, or whispered promises in this bed can mend it all tonight.

Chapter Thirteen

Day Five

Scott

Sunlight filters through the slatted shutters of the bungalow, soft and gold, turning the room into something almost peaceful. Lyla is still asleep against my chest. Her cheek presses to my skin. One arm drapes loosely across my ribs. Her breathing is slow, even, steady in a way that makes my heart stutter, remembering how it used to match mine years ago.

I don't move. Don't dare. Last night cracked something open between us—grief, truth, bodies finally saying what words never could. For the first time since the show started, I let myself feel something close to hope. Cautious. Fragile. One night doesn't erase ten years of silence, doesn't rebuild the trust I'd shattered when I walked away.

She lost a child because of me. Her entire world was turned upside down because of me. It's no wonder she doesn't trust me. I wouldn't trust me.

But her head on my chest feels like proof we aren't starting from nothing.

I trace the line of her shoulder with my thumb—barely touching, just enough to feel her warmth. Her hair smells like rain, salt, and us. I close my eyes and let the moment stretch, knowing it won't last.

Lyla stirs. Her lashes flutter. For a second, she's still, eyes fixed on my collarbone, as if she's processing whether last night was real or a dream she can still wake from.

Then awareness hits. Her body goes taut. She doesn't pull away, but she doesn't melt into me again either. I feel the shift in her breath, the subtle tightening of muscles that were loose seconds ago.

I speak softly to her. "Morning."

She swallows. "Morning."

We stay frozen for a long moment. Her fingers flex against my side, then still.

"Oh, my god, we..." she whispers, almost to herself.

"Yeah." I keep my hand light on her back. "We did."

She glances around, like she's bracing for impact.

"But it mattered," I add quietly. "More than you know."

Her gaze lifts. Searching, conflicted. As if the truth I gave her last night is reshaping everything she thought she knew about me, about us. Her brows pinch. She bites the inside of her cheek, no doubt reconciling the man holding her with the one who disappeared.

She doesn't speak. Instead, she shifts slightly, her cheek on my shoulder. I feel her inhale, slow and deliberate, like she's stealing one last breath of me before reality pulls me back.

I press my lips to her hair. "I'm not going anywhere," I whisper.

She doesn't answer, but doesn't pull away.

We stay tangled until the distant thrum of helicopter blades slices the quiet. First faint, then louder.

Our bubble has officially been burst.

Lyla tenses. "That's our ride."

"Yeah."

She eases out of my arms. I let her go, watching as she sits up. The sheet pools around her waist. Sunlight catches the faint marks I left on her skin. Nothing harsh, just echoes of last night's reverence.

She reaches for her sundress on the floor and shakes it out. I grab my shorts and shirt nearby. We dress in fragile silence, as though speaking too loud will shatter what's left.

At the bed's edge, she pauses, fingers twisting the hem of her dress. "Scott..."

I look up.

"Thank you," she says, a small smile flickering on her face. "For last night. For telling me everything."

I nod. "I'm sorry it took us this long."

Her eyes flicker. Something raw passes through them. Then she looks away. "We should go."

Every step toward the door feels mechanical, pulling us from tangled sheets and whispered confessions.

Outside, the helicopter waits, rotors spinning lazily. A producer waves us over with a tablet. She looks to be relieved when she sees us.

"Oh, good, you two are still alive," she says brightly, schooling her expression to a smile that doesn't reach her eyes. "Ready to head back?"

Lyla nods. I place a hand on the small of her back, guiding. She doesn't flinch but doesn't lean in, either.

When we climb in, the door seals behind us. The chopper lifts off with the bungalow shrinking below.

Lyla shifts immediately and presses against the opposite door, staring out at the ocean like it holds answers my face can't give.

I watch her retreat, my chest aching like a fresh bruise. This is what I've reduced her to: a woman so terrified of abandonment she's already running before I've left.

The producer drones on through headsets—weather, producer complaints about no footage last night. I tune it out. All I see is Lyla's shallow breathing, rigid shoulders, and careful distance.

She's going to choose Damon.

The realization should destroy me. But underneath the pain, clarity surfaces.

She doesn't trust I'll stay. She doesn't need promises or words. She needs proof. And the only proof that matters is action.

If I fight her choice, I prove I don't respect her judgment. But if I leave, would that only prove her point? Just watching her with another man, even so much as the thought of it, is unbearable. Leaving for that reason would only prove her fears right.

Maybe the only way to break the cycle is to stay. To respect her choice and hope she comes back on her own. To be present every day, even when it's torture, until she realizes I'm not going anywhere.

Fuck.

Keeping my distance was already torture enough. But now that I've had her under me—touched her, smelled her skin, heard her laugh—I can't fathom letting someone else, Damon, touch what's mine.

Losing her once was torture. Losing her again, and probably for good if that happens, is worse than any agony.

Five minutes pass. Ten. Silence stretches like an open wound.

"You're going to choose him," I say. That's not me demanding. It's just fact.

Her shoulders tense, but she doesn't turn. "I don't know."

"You will." I keep my voice level despite the clawing in my chest. "Because he's never left you. And I have."

"Scott—"

"I'm not asking you to change your mind." The words burn. "But I need you to hear this. You're going to choose him. Anything to make you feel safe."

She finally looks at me— Eyes wide, a tear spills.

"But I'm staying," I say. "If you choose him. If he kisses you on camera. Even if you're in his bed. I'm still going to be here."

"Why would you—"

"You need to know if you can trust me to not abandon you." I hold her gaze. "So here it is. Push me away. Test me. Do what you have to in order to get the answers you need."

She stares at me like I've lost my mind.

Maybe I have.

"You're terrified the past will repeat." I lean closer to her. Her eyes are filled with trepidation. "This is me saying it won't."

The skids touch down. She unbuckles fast and climbs out without waiting.

I watch her disappear into the swarm of women—hugs, questions, laughter.

And I know with devastating certainty what I've just set in motion.

~

Lyla

Every time I close my eyes, I see Scott's face. The raw pain when he spoke about his father's threats, the crack in his voice when he said leaving me was the hardest thing he'd ever done.

Vincent Bennett threatened to destroy my family if Scott didn't end us.

The truth has looped in my head since I woke up on his chest this morning. It changes everything. He didn't leave because he got bored with me or thought the grass would be greener on the other side. He left to protect me.

But anger still simmers beneath the understanding. Not at his choice—I can see the impossible position his father forced him into—but at the secrecy. At ten years believing the worst of him, believing I wasn't worth fighting for, when the truth was so much more complicated.

On the helicopter ride back, he wanted to be close to me. I secretly craved more—his hand on mine, his arm around me, anything to keep the fragile warmth of last night alive. But I couldn't let myself take it. The moment the skids touched down and the doors opened, I bolted. Straight to the pool deck. Away from him. Away from the careful politeness we've both been clinging to since dawn, when his hands were still on my skin and every reason to resist him disappeared.

God, the way he made me feel.

Even now, the memory sends heat pooling low. His mouth worshipping me, claiming me like a man starved. For those hours, I'd been his completely—no walls, just raw need and connection.

And that terrifies me more than his abandonment ever did.

Because if I let him back in that deep again, in my body, my soul, and he leaves—even for the right reasons—it will break me beyond repair.

"You look like hell," Emily says as we settle into a quieter corner of the villa. We stretch out in sun chairs facing the blinding tropical horizon. I don't look at her, but I hear the sympathy threaded through her bluntness.

"Thanks. Exactly what every woman wants to hear."

"I call it like I see it." She studies me with the directness that made us fast friends. "Want to talk about it?"

The offer hangs between us, tempting. I've carried this alone for less than twenty-four hours, and the weight of it already feels crushing.

"It's complicated."

"The best things usually are." Emily leans back, sunglasses hiding her eyes. "Try me. I'm a good listener."

Where do I start?

The boy who loved me enough to sacrifice everything?

The man who kept me in the dark for my *protection?*

Or the terrifying truth that I want him again?

"Scott told me why he left," I say finally.

"And?"

The words spill out—Vincent's threats, Scott's impossible choice, ten years built on a lie. Emily doesn't interrupt once. Her expression shifts slowly from shock to thoughtfulness.

"Holy shit," she breathes when I finish. "That's...romantic in the most fucked-up way I've ever heard."

"Romantic?" I stare at her. "He made a life-altering decision without me. Let me believe our relationship meant nothing."

"You were both kids," Emily says quietly. "You can't expect an eighteen-year-old to go to war with his father and come out knowing exactly what the right move is."

I shake my head.

"If you really think about it," she continues, "leaving was his way of fighting back. I'd be saying something very different if he'd dumped you like his dad told him to."

"He still left."

Emily nods slowly. "That's true. And I can't imagine how much that hurt you back then. But you deserved the truth, even if it was ugly. He did the right thing telling you."

"He's been trying to explain since the first day we got here. And I kept pushing him away, convinced whatever reason he had would just be some lousy excuse."

If I'd let him explain sooner...would anything be different?

Maybe it would have changed everything. Maybe nothing at all. I'll never know. But the important thing is that I know now.

"Hate what he did all you want," Emily says gently, "but you have to admit how much he gave up."

She squeezes my hand.

"His life with you. His home. And staying completely silent for ten years just to keep you safe? That's not a man who didn't care. That's a man who cared too much and believed silence was the only way to protect you."

Tears prick my eyes.

"You're allowed to be angry about that silence," she continues softly. "God knows I would be. I can't imagine what you've carried all those years by yourself. But don't hate him for something he had no control over."

"That's the thing." My voice comes out quieter than I expect. "I can't hate him. Not anymore."

Emily hesitates, like she's weighing whether to ask the next question.

"What happened over there?" she finally asks. "The crew was freaking out when we lost power—especially when your mics went dead."

If they don't know now, it's probably best they never do.

"Last night..." I swallow. "God, Emily. I've never felt anything like that." Heat creeps up my neck even thinking about it. "And it scares the hell out of me."

I stare out at the endless stretch of ocean.

"But I still want him."

She exhales slowly. "If you let him back in—and history repeats itself, no matter the reason—you're afraid of getting hurt all over again."

She reads me like an open book.

I nod, my throat tight.

She takes both my hands in hers. "Here's the thing. Forgiveness isn't about erasing the pain. It's about deciding if the man in front of you is worth the risk. The longer he stays here, the longer he fights for you—even if you choose someone else—the more proof he's giving you."

"But what if that proof is only temporary?" Anxiety twists tighter in my chest.

"Lyla, sweetie," Emily squeezes my fingers. "You don't have to decide everything right this second. For now, until he fully proves himself to you, protect your heart. But don't shut him out completely. Just...watch him. Observe."

I turn my gaze back to the water stretching endlessly ahead of us. Sunlight scatters across the ripples.

"What if I choose wrong?"

"There's risk in everything we do. That's just life." She shrugs lightly. "And if it turns out you did choose wrong? Then you choose again. Except for death, almost nothing in this world is permanent." She studies me for a moment longer. "But don't choose out of fear. Choose the man—whoever he ends up being—because you want him. Because the risk feels worth it." She stands, squeezing my shoulder. "I'm here if you ever need someone to listen. No matter what."

As she walks away, I sit there with her words.

My heart feels torn. Torn between safety...and the terrifying pull of him. And the only decisions I feel capable of making are to take a long shower and put on fresh clothes.

Chapter Fourteen

Lyla

Despite the scalding shower and clean clothes, my skin still feels branded.

Emily's words won't stop looping, low and relentless like the tide dragging sand from under my feet. *Hate what he did all you want, but you have to admit how much he gave up.* Vincent's threats. The impossible choice Scott made at eighteen. The way his body had felt like coming home and a free fall at the same time—hard muscle, rough hands, that low growl against my throat when he'd pinned me last night and rasped *You're still mine.*

What could have been. What still is.

But sacrifice doesn't equal safety. Not here. Not when every camera is hungry and the show keeps rewriting the rules just to watch us bleed.

The wooden platform creaks beneath my sandals as the rest of us gather. Salt wind snaps at my pink tee and shorts, plastering the thin cotton to my chest and hips like a second skin. I cross my arms, pretending it's the breeze and not the memory of Scott's hands that has my nipples tightening.

Miranda steps forward, white linen practically glowing against the emerald palm trees behind her, smile sharp enough to cut glass.

"Today's challenge will be all about collaboration and communication," she announces, voice bright as fresh-cut pineapple and twice as dangerous. "But there's a twist. You won't be paired with your current... *couplings*." She pauses for the cameras to zoom. "Gentleman, you'll draw names at random from this velvet bag."

My stomach drops like a stone. I lock my expression into neutral, eyes fixed on the bag as if it's wired to detonate. Damon reaches in first. His fingers disappear, then reappear with a slip of paper. That easy, sun-bleached grin spreads across his face.

"Lyla."

I can't help it— I glance at Scott.

His jaw flexes once, sharp and controlled, but his eyes... God, his eyes. They darken to storm-cloud blue, raw possessiveness flashing hot enough to scorch me from ten feet away—the exact same look he wore last night right before he had me pinned, breathless, whispering filthy promises against my mouth. My thighs clench on instinct.

Traitor.

I force my legs to move anyway. Damon's hand settles lightly at the small of my back as I step up beside him—steady, polite, nothing like the way Scott's grip had branded me last night.

"I'm glad you're okay," Damon murmurs, warm breath brushing my ear. "How are you feeling, really?"

Forget the bag. His loaded question might as well be a live grenade.

I force a smile. "It went great."

If you call a devastating confession from your ex followed by mind-blowing sex great.

I turn away from him before he can dig deeper. The last thing I need is this conversation going anywhere near last night.

Scott draws next. He doesn't even look at the slip. His gaze cuts straight across the circle—steady, deliberate, scorching—locking onto mine like he's already claiming me. Then his voice drops, low and rough.

"Valerie."

Valerie steps forward with a delighted little laugh that floats over the group like she's already won the whole damn show. Hips swaying, golden skin glowing under the sun, every inch the confident woman who knows exactly how to get a man. Something hot and ugly twists low in my stomach. I shove it down hard, trying not to think about it. Not to let it consume me. At least for now.

When every pair is locked in, Miranda claps, all sunshine and shark teeth.

"Rules are simple. You're tied at the waist with a three-foot rope. Cross the course together without letting it go taut. No pulling. No extra touching. First pair through without penalties wins a private terrace dinner tonight—and the lucky lady wins an advantage at tomorrow's coupling ceremony. And that is once she chooses the man she wants to couple up with, her choice can't be stolen or vetoed. Not even by the man himself. Let's see who can actually move as one."

The course is a relay style race with seven rows, highlighted in white chalk from one side of the field to the other about the length of half a football field. A few beams are spread throughout, enough to hold two people at once, but barely.

Damon and I get clipped together. The rope sits too low on my hips. Intimate in the worst way, the rough hemp brushing the bare skin just above my shorts. His fingers graze my waist while he adjusts the knot, gentle, almost apologetic. "We've got this," he murmurs, voice light and easy. "Just stay with me."

We don't.

His directions come quick but loose. "Slow down—wait, match my step—" We lurch forward, competent enough to stay upright, but every sync feels off by a fatal half-second. The rope snaps tight again and again, jerking us to a stop, yanking my body into his. Each tug feels like a punishment. Like the universe is laughing at how wrong this fit is.

Miranda's voice cuts through the chaos like a whip.

"Damon and Lyla's rope went taut—back to the start!"

We're sent to the starting line twice more before we even clear a third of the field. My skin prickles with the wrongness of it all—Damon's steady hand at my back, his easy laugh when we stumble. Safe.

Kind. Nothing like the man whose voice I can already hear slicing through the noise, calm and lethal.

Scott.

"Valerie, left foot first. Match my pace exactly. Breathe with me. Good. Now step—higher on the beam. Trust the rope. I've got you."

His commands are quiet, precise, wrapped in that same velvet-steel authority that made my knees buckle last night when he had me pinned under him. I *know* that tone. Know exactly how it feels when it's aimed at me—controlled, intentional, impossible to ignore. My pulse stutters. My thighs clench around the memory of his growl against my throat.

Valerie's replies come breathy and eager, like she's melting under every syllable. "Like this?"

The seed of jealousy that started as a flicker now coils tight and vicious in my belly, sharp enough to draw blood. I hate it. I hate *her*. I hate how perfectly they move together.

When Miranda finally calls time, Damon and I are still at the starting line, rope snapping taut between us, frustration thick enough to choke on. My fingers shake as I unclip.

"Scott and Valerie win!" Miranda crows, all glitter and triumph.

Valerie is flushed and laughing, glowing like she just won more than a dinner. Scott stands tall and unruffled, the rope slack between them as if it never dared to fight them once. Not a drop of sweat. Not a single misstep. She beams, shoulder brushing Scott's chest as she tilts her head up at him—proud, pleased, possessive. He doesn't move away. Just gives her one controlled nod.

My chest tightens so hard I feel it in my ribs.

Suddenly every eye is on me. The cameras zoom in like vultures. Everyone's already assuming Scott will pick me in the coupling ceremony. And ten minutes ago, I would have believed it too...except for the way Valerie's smile looks more than friendly. Like she already knows exactly how this night is going to end.

I can't look away from them—his tall frame still radiating that quiet, lethal dominance, Valerie glowing beside him like she belongs there. The same man Emily swore gave up everything for me once.

Chapter Fifteen

Day 5 (evening)

Scott

The terrace smells like jasmine and citronella, and someone else's idea of romance.

String lights loop overhead, warm and deliberate. Two chairs are pulled close together at a small table. Close enough that knees would touch if one of us lean in. A bottle of wine already open, already breathing. Candles in glass votives, flames barely moving in the still evening air. A producer walked me through it forty minutes ago with the enthusiasm of someone staging a listing. *The crew will be just off camera. Try to enjoy yourselves. This is your moment.*

My moment...right. Like I wanted this moment with someone that wasn't with Lyla to begin with.

I sit, taking in the view. The ocean slowly going dark as the last of the sun dissolves and disappears into the horizon. A reminder to myself that I only have five days left. Five days left until real life comes knocking. A life where none of this exists and the only thing that matters is whether Lyla will let me in. And once money isn't hanging over her head anymore, she'll no doubt try to get as far away from me as possible.

Right now, this date isn't helping.

Valerie arrives moments later. She's made an effort. Her hair is down, resting on exposed shoulders as she wears a yellow dress that catches the light when she moves. She smiles when she sees me, and it's a real smile—wide, a little nervous, the kind of smile that says this moment means something to her. That's the part that makes this harder. She isn't performing.

"You clean up well," she says, settling into the chair across from me.

"You, too."

She laughs, reaching for the wine and pouring us both a glass without asking. I register it the way I register everything—noted, filed, and nothing of consequence.

Somewhere behind her head, a camera shifts.

Valerie seems like a sweet girl, easy to talk to. She's funny when she's not trying to be, quick with an opinion, doesn't fill silence with noise just to fill it. The right guy would be lucky to be sitting where I am. That's just not me.

My heart belongs to Lyla, and that's not going to change.

She asks about my work. Security, I tell her. Private sector now, Marines before that. I leave out my complicated past. She then asks what made me leave the Corps, and I give her the honest version but keep it short and sweet. Her questions then become mundane like what I do on days off. I choose a simple response.

"Fishing," I say. "If I can get to Grapevine Lake."

"I didn't picture you as patient enough for fishing."

"Most people don't." I turn my glass once. "It's not about the fish."

She leans in slightly, elbows on the table and her head resting on her hands. "What's it about then?"

"Quiet."

Before she can respond, the food comes. Grilled fish, rice, and sliced mango—someone put actual thought into it.

We eat. She talks about her family, her two younger brothers out in Phoenix, and her mother who calls her every Sunday. She says it like it's a complaint, but the warmth underneath it is obvious.

Somewhere in the middle of her speaking, I zone out thinking about Lyla. About the space between us since coming back to the villa. About how I'd rather fill that space right now than be here.

Valerie is kind, but she's barking up the wrong tree.

I pick up my glass.

"Can I ask you something?" Valerie says.

"Sure."

"Why are you here?" She says it without accusation, genuine curiosity rather than prying. "Everyone around here has a different idea, and I'd rather ask the source. You don't come off as the typical TV personality."

I shake my head. "I'm not."

She sobers. "You're here for Lyla, aren't you?"

I nod.

She tilts her head, processing—fitting it into whatever version of me she's been constructing.

"Do you think she wants you back?"

The candle between us shivers once.

"The question isn't does she. It's *whether* she will take me back."

"That's confident," she observes. "What makes you think that?"

"Let's just say Lyla and I go way back."

She scoffs. "You and everyone else here."

Her smile falters, softening into something more polite. I can see her rearranging something internally. She reaches for the wine bottle and tops off my glass, then hers, without saying anything else.

By the time the plates are cleared, the sky is fully dark. Stars come through, close and heavy, the way they only get out here, away from everything. Valerie turns her face up to look at them.

"This part I'll miss," she speaks softly. "The sky."

"Yeah."

She looks back down. Looks at me. There's a shift in her expression, as though she's decided something.

She then stands and leans across the corner of the table. I recognize what she's trying to do.

I'm quick to pull back, one hand gentle at her shoulder.

My lips land at her cheekbone—brief, unambiguous. A press. Nothing more. The kind of kiss you give a sibling, not a potential significant other.

Her eyes open. She's perfectly still for a moment, as if processing the message I'm giving her.

Then she blinks and settles back into her chair. A soft exhale through her nose.

"Oh," she says, heat crawling up her face. "You weren't kidding about Lyla."

"Valerie."

"No, it's—" She shakes her head, a small rueful curve at the corner of her mouth. Not angry. Just recalibrating. "I read that wrong."

"You're—" I want to be honest, because she deserves that much.

"Don't." She holds up a hand, and there's a quiet laugh underneath it, as though she's laughing to herself. "Please don't finish that sentence. I already feel embarrassed enough."

I close my mouth.

She looks out at the water for a moment. The embarrassment settles and what's left underneath is two people without pretense between them for the first time all evening.

But what if I could use this time with Valerie to my advantage? What if I gave her an opportunity where we both could possibly get what we want? What if I got her to choose Damon in the coupling ceremony? She's beholden to no other guy here, and there's zero chance her ex will have the balls to even reconcile with her.

I lean forward. "Can I ask you something?"

She glances back. "After all that, I might as well be an open book."

"Tomorrow. Your first pick." I hold her gaze. "What do you think of Damon?"

She stares at me for a long moment. "I haven't given him much thought. Why?"

"I just think you two would have more in common." I don't know that for sure. It's a hunch, but one I'm willing to work to my advantage.

Then she laughs. Not harshly, but with the full weight of disbelief behind it. "You're asking me to hand my advantage to someone else?"

She caught on quick.

"I'm asking you to consider it."

She hesitates. "For Lyla."

"For you, too," I say. "Damon seems like a good guy. He might surprise you. Just sleep on it."

She leans back in her chair, arms crossing loosely, thinking. Her eyes move to the candle between us.

"You know," she says slowly, "most men would've just let me pick them and figured they'd sort the rest out later, once I became another notch on their bedpost."

"You deserve better. And I'm not most men."

"No." She exhales. "You really aren't."

Silence falls between us. The ocean fills the silence, low and constant beyond the terrace railing.

"I'll think about it," she says finally.

She's not saying yes. But her response isn't a no either, and I know better than to push further. I nod once and let it sit.

She closes her eyes for a moment, taking in deep breaths as if composing herself with a dignity I respect. Then she meets my eyes across the candles.

"She's lucky," she says.

I think back to Lyla on that helicopter. Shoulder to shoulder. Eyes forward.

"I know. She just doesn't know that yet," I say.

Valerie holds my gaze for a long moment.

"She should."

After dinner is over, we walk back to the others, side by side, without saying much else. Side by side. Cameras track us the whole way.

Inside, the common area is loud with conversation and music.

Valerie's words echo in my mind. *I'll think about it.*

They're not enough to count on, especially when Valerie owes me nothing. I sealed that fact the moment I rejected her kiss. Whatever she decides tomorrow, she'll decide it for herself, and she'd be right to. I just hope she takes me into account, not just Damon.

Somewhere in this villa, Lyla is thinking about me, about us. I know it the same way I've always known things about her. It's not logical, just a gut feeling. I'd be an idiot not to think she's turning over what we talked about. That she's building her walls back up brick by careful brick.

And if that's true, and she ends up choosing Damon despite my efforts, I don't know what I'll do.

Chapter Sixteen

Lyla

The outdoor lounge is scattered with drinks, half-faked laughter, and the low hum of cameras that never really turn off. Warm string lights shimmer over the pool, turning every ripple of water into liquid gold—designed, I'm sure, to make emotional breakdowns entertaining.

I'm curled into the corner of the sectional, pretending to sip a drink that tastes like nothing. Damon sits beside me, close but never touching, his steady presence usually a balm. Tonight, it only makes the tension under my skin feel sharper, like a live wire humming too close to water.

Conversation drifts the way it always does this late—loose, aimless, everyone filling the silence because nobody wants to look boring on cable television.

Ava saunters in from the production hallway, fresh drink in hand and the glossy-eyed energy of someone who's just found out something juicy. She drops onto the chair across from us, legs crossed, lips already curving.

"Okay." She scans the group with a satisfied little smirk. "Has anyone else wandered past the monitor bank in the back hallway?"

A few people shrug, mild interest at best.

"Scott and Valerie." Ava raises her brows, letting the names hang like bait. "I only caught a little bit of it, but I just gotta say... That private terrace setup did *not* go to waste."

I freeze. Ice slides down my spine and pools low in my belly. My chest burns.

"Girl, spill," Kylie demands.

Ava takes a slow, theatrical sip. "Valerie shot her shot. And from what I saw on the feed"—she pauses just long enough for the group to lean in—"it was getting *spicy*."

Laughter ripples. Someone whoops. Another calls Valerie *bold,* like it's a compliment instead of a knife.

I stare at the condensation sliding down my glass, watching droplets race each other the way my pulse is racing in my throat. The words sink in slowly, as if cold water was filling my lungs—not a shock, but a gradual, suffocating chill.

Underneath the hurt, something uglier blooms. Jealousy so sharp it tastes metallic. Because for one stupid night, I let myself believe every word he growled against my skin. *It mattered. More than you know.*

I should have known better.

A decade of scars, and I still let him split me open again with nothing but that velvety voice and those strong, sure hands. Now I'm right back where I swore I'd never be—falling into pieces while he's somewhere at a candlelight dinner, no doubt with another woman's mouth on his.

To think I'd sworn I'd never let myself feel this way again.

I'm older, but apparently no wiser.

I force my face into a neutral expression and take a slow sip of my drink, which tastes more like ash with each second that passes.

"Lyla." Emily's voice is soft, close. She crouches beside my knees, eyes searching mine.

I flash her the smile I've perfected for brides who are one wrong napkin shade away from a meltdown—small, bright, bulletproof. But Emily doesn't blink. Her expression doesn't change.

"I'm okay," I lie, throat tightening around the words. "Really."

She stays quiet, rubbing slow circles on my arm like she's waiting for the dam to crack. For one weak second, I almost lean in. Almost let the sting behind my eyes spill over.

Then anger surges—hot, clean, aimed squarely at myself—and I straighten.

"It's nothing," I assure her, turning back toward the pool. "He's just a guy."

She doesn't believe me, but she lets it go. The conversation drifts on around us. Ava has already moved on, gossip spent, the group laughing about something else like my entire world didn't just tilt on its axis.

Footsteps echo on the stone stairs. Someone whistles low.

Valerie appears first, stunning in a sunshine-yellow dress, skin vibrant with a sun-kissed glow. She looks to Scott, smiling, as though she enjoyed being with him tonight. Scott walks a step behind her, steady, composed, the ghost of a satisfied smirk tugging at the corner of his mouth.

Seeing them together is like a punch that has landed right between my ribs. My breath catches so hard; the glass trembles in my hand.

Valerie peels off toward the group, instantly swallowed by the chorus of "How was it?" and "Tell us everything!" She sinks into a chair with effortless confidence.

"It was great," she announces, voice honey sweet. "I enjoyed our time together."

"And Scott?" someone teases.

She glances back at him, grinning like they share a secret. "Surprisingly...tolerable."

Laughter ripples through the lounge. Scott gives a silent nod, eyes scanning the group—until they lock on mine.

My mind swarms with every awful question I've been avoiding all night.

Is he moving on?

Did he think of me the whole time?

Or did he forget I existed the second she came into view?

A sick wave rolls through my stomach, hot and sour. I told myself I was prepared. Told myself distance was best. But one look at him and that tether between us yanks tight around my heart.

I tear my gaze away.

Damon nudges my knee, voice low. "You good?"

"I'm fine." My smile is plastic, but it doesn't fool him. His brow lifts, knowing. He doesn't push. Smart man.

Miranda sweeps in like she's been waiting for blood in the water, clapping her hands with bright, predatory glee. "Group debrief! Highs, lows, awkward moments, romantic sparks—everything. Cameras are rolling!"

The collective groan could rattle the palm trees.

Of course she wants our psyches on display.

Valerie goes first, keeping her responses vague and surface-level. Food, view, ambiance. Warm but noncommittal. Nothing that would give the editors too much to work with.

Then Miranda's gaze clicks onto me like a sniper scope. "Lyla, you're someone who builds other people's love stories for a living. Watching one potentially unfold tonight... What does that stir up for you?"

The question lands hard. If there weren't twelve lenses pointed at my face, I'd rather answer with a slap across her Botoxed cheek. Instead, I straighten and smooth my expression into the same calm I use on hysterical brides.

"Honestly?" My voice comes out sugar-sweet and razor sharp. "I think it's great. Some people need to explore every shiny new option before they figure out what they actually want." I let my eyes flick to Scott for half a second. "Watching someone chase that? It's the most familiar thing I've seen all week. But I learned a long time ago not to hold my breath waiting for the process to finish."

A sliver of vicious pride flares in my chest.

That felt good.

Scott's jaw tightens. He seems...alarmed. Like he just heard what I said, and his first instinct is to immediately know why. His eyes find mine, searching, frantic, like he's trying to trace the damage back to its source. For a suspended second, he looks ready to stand up and drag me somewhere private.

I don't give him the chance, tearing my gaze away before he can speak.

Whatever that look means, I'm not interested.

Fool me once, shame on him. Fool me twice...

Miranda looks satisfied and moves on.

Thank God.

The debrief wraps a few minutes later. The others scatter toward their own suites, the night air thick with humidity and unspoken drama.

"I'm calling it," I announce, pushing to my feet. "I'm exhausted."

I need to crawl into the suite I share with Scott and force sleep to shut my brain off before I do something stupid like cry.

"Want me to walk with you?" Damon asks, already rising.

We fall into step. The night air is humid with a light breeze, but it does nothing to settle the storm inside me.

A long stretch of silence passes before he speaks, voice gentle but direct. "We haven't really talked since you got back from your unexpected night with Scott."

Unexpected *would be an understatement.*

My steps falter for half a second.

He keeps walking, eyes on the path ahead like he's simply stating facts. "I've been watching you tonight. You're in your head. Distant. Like you're carrying something you're not ready to face."

Heat crawls up my neck. "Damon—"

"I'm not pushing for answers tonight," he cuts in calmly, still patient, steady. "I'm just saying I see it. And I'm still here. I still want to see where this goes between us." He glances over, expression open and level. "I know we've only known each other for a few days, but we click, Lyla. We enjoy each other's company without the unnecessary drama or fireworks. That's enough for me, and I think it's what you've been wanting, too. I'm not going anywhere just because things got complicated."

The words land like a quiet boundary and a reminder all at once.

"I'm not trying to hurt you or lead you on," I whisper.

"I know." He stops at the entrance to my suite. "Just make sure you're choosing for the right reasons. Not because of him. Not because of the cameras. And not because you're worried about wasting my time."

What are those reasons anymore?

Would coupling up with Damon give me clarity like I thought? Would he help me realize what I want, or would it do the exact opposite?

Damon is in every way, shape, and form what I need—on paper. There is absolutely *nothing* wrong with him. But what he's asking is compatibility before passion. Why does that not feel quite right?

So why, after watching Scott with Valerie, does safe suddenly feel like it's not enough? Why does seeing Scott move on hurt more than it should?

Chapter Seventeen

Day Six

Scott

I'm twenty yards behind them on the torch-lit path, flip-flop-dressed feet silent out of habit, when I see Damon's hand on the suite doorframe. Lyla is already inside, the soft click of the latch cutting off the night like a guillotine. He's still standing there—tall, stable, the kind of guy who could make a woman feel safe just by the sound of his voice.

Fuck no.

I keep walking.

He must hear me coming because then he turns in my direction. Our eyes meet under the low glow of the villa sconces. No words are exchanged. No words needed. His expression doesn't change—calm, patient, like he's already decided this isn't a fight he's going to lose tonight. Deep down, the caveman in me would rather rip him apart with my bare hands than let him anywhere near her.

He nods once, civil. "She's inside."

I don't thank him. I don't need to. I get the message he's sending. *I'm not backing down. You want her? Earn her.*

He steps aside without another word, disappearing down the path.

I push open the door.

Only a single lamp on the far nightstand is lit softly, enveloping the room in a soft ambiance of warm light. Lyla is at the bathroom mirror, face half turned away, working a brush through her hair with the focused energy of someone who heard the door and decided not to acknowledge it.

I close the door behind me. The latch clicks like a starting gun as she continues brushing.

I pull off my watch and set it on the dresser. The silence between us is filled with tension—and not the kind we'd found in the bungalow the night before. This is loaded, deadly. I run back through the evening trying to locate the source of it and come up empty.

I try to make small talk first. "How was your night?"

"Fine."

One harsh-sounding word.

This doesn't look good.

"You left the debrief fast."

"I was tired."

No, she wasn't.

She's been tired the way people are tired when they don't want to be in the same room as you. With Lyla, I know when I'm on the receiving end of that specific kind of tired.

I lean against the doorframe of the bathroom, arms loose at my sides. She doesn't look up.

"Little one."

"I'm getting ready for bed, Scott."

"I can see that." I keep my voice even. "I can tell something's off. So let's not pretend this elephant in the room isn't here."

She sets the brush down on the counter with a quiet click. Picking up her moisturizer, she opens it and takes her time with the cap.

"Nothing's off," she says to the mirror. "It was a long day."

"It was." I watch her hands move, methodical, unhurried. "And now you won't look at me."

At my words, her hands slow for a fraction of a second before resuming.

"I'm looking at myself," she says. "Some of us have a skincare routine."

"Talk to me, little one," I speak softly. "Whatever it is."

For a moment, she meets my eyes in the mirror finally.

"How was your date?"

"It was fine," I reply. "Dinner. Conversation. Nothing worth reporting."

"Mmm." She goes back to the mirror. "Funny. Valerie didn't look like a woman who had a forgettable evening."

"What did Valerie say?"

She turns then, crossing her arms. Eyes level. "It wasn't Valerie." She pauses. "Does it matter who said what?"

Translation: someone said something.

I run through the evening in my head—the group reconvening, the debrief, the way everyone stared between me, Lyla, and Valerie like fresh gossip—

It's a hunch, but...

"Whatever you heard," I say carefully, "I'd like the chance to tell you what actually happened."

"What actually happened." She repeats flatly. Not a question.

"Yes."

"And what actually happened, Scott?"

"We had dinner. She tried to kiss me." I hold her gaze. "I didn't let her."

Something shifts slightly in her expression. As though she's working the information through her mind.

"I redirected it," I explain. "It wasn't what it probably looked like on a monitor."

"A monitor." Her eyes sharpen slightly. So she does know about the monitors. "You're guessing an awful lot about what I heard."

"I'm guessing because you won't tell me what you know," I point out, pushing off the doorframe and taking one measured step into the bathroom. Not close enough to touch her, but close enough that my reflection fills the mirror beside her. "Which means whatever it was hit hard enough that you'd rather stay angry than give me a chance to explain it."

She exhales deeply. "I'm not angry."

"No," I agree. "You're hurt. Which is worse."

The silence that follows is different from the ones before it. Longer. She looks at me with something behind her eyes that she's working very hard to hide.

"It doesn't matter," she says finally.

"It does."

"Scott—"

"Let me finish."

She closes her mouth, eyes narrowed.

"I don't want Valerie." I hold her gaze and don't let her look away from it. "I didn't want her at dinner. I didn't want her when she leaned across the table. I redirected her kiss because there is no version of this where I want anyone in this villa except you." I pause. "That doesn't stop being true because you're angry at me."

Something flashes through her expression. Gone before I can name it.

"You don't have to believe me tonight," I say quietly. "But I need you to have heard it."

She looks at me for a long moment. The lamp light catches the edge of her face, the careful stillness she's maintaining with both hands.

Then—

"Go to bed, Scott."

She turns back to the mirror.

I stand there another second, reading her the way I've always been able to read her even when she doesn't want to be read. The way she turned back to the mirror instead of to the door. The deliberate quality of her stillness. She's not dismissing me. She's keeping me at arm's length until she decides what to do next.

"Goodnight, Lyla."

I pull the bathroom door halfway closed behind me and sit on the couch in the half dark. The tap turns, followed by the cabinet clicking shut. Her lamp goes off.

Then quiet.

I stare at the ceiling and hold onto the crack in her facade I saw. That half second where something got through before she closed it back up. Whether it's still standing in the morning, whether she carries it into that ceremony or buries it— I won't know until I see her face in the morning.

~

Day 7 (morning)

Lyla

The terrace has been transformed overnight into something deliberately romantic. Hibiscus petals are scattered across the stone, the ocean glittering behind us, the morning light soft as though it was considered in the design like a paid actor. Everyone is gathered in a loose semicircle, dressed and present, the air carrying that particular charged stillness of people bracing for whatever new drama will inevitably unfold.

I stand between Emily and Kylie with my hands loosely clasped and Scott's words from last night still turning over in my head.

I don't want Valerie... There is no version of this where I want anyone in this villa except you.

Maybe Ava didn't have the whole picture. She saw, what, thirty seconds of footage? And through a monitor no less. She filled in the rest herself, the way people do when a story is more interesting than the truth.

That's plausible.

But then Valerie walked back with Scott in tow—and the particular warmth of a woman who'd had a good evening—and that image can't just disappear simply because Scott says nothing happened.

So I don't know. That's the honest answer. I don't know what will happen or what I'm going to do.

My eyes scan the semicircle, from one nervous face to the next.

Scott, in a white dress shirt that makes his eyes impossibly bluer, stands with the other men, hands in his pockets, weight slightly forward. He finds me the moment I look—like he could sense I was staring. He holds eye contact with that sure expression that has been dismantling me since the first day on this beach. Like he has nothing to hide and everything to prove.

I look away first and move my gaze to Damon just a few men down the line. His presence is eye-catching in a stark black dress shirt and pants, his stoicism radiating across the distance between us. He's somewhat intimidating, intense, but perhaps underneath lies a deeper vulnerability than he's willing to show. His eyes soften when they meet mine. They're kind and thoughtful, but the connection he's trying to capture in his gaze feels distant. Like I'm following a string on the ground, only to realize a brick wall blocks my path and I can't move forward.

On paper, Damon makes perfect sense. He's consistent, responsive, understanding, and asking nothing emotionally that I'm not already prepared to give. But every time I try to picture settling into that life with him, I run up against the same hollow feeling I can't explain away, no matter how many reasonable arguments I make with myself. As though something is missing, a piece of him that I'm unable to reach, and I've been ignoring that feeling since our first date.

Out of all the other women here, he'd chosen me. Isn't that enough to settle with?

Miranda steps forward into the center of the semicircle.

"Good morning. Today is our coupling ceremony. Soon, we're going to find out where we all truly stand." She pauses. "Before we begin, a reminder about the advantage earned in yesterday's challenge. Valerie has an advantage that will allow her to make her choice without any steal or veto. That extends not just to the other women choosing, but also her chosen partner."

Around me, the group seems to absorb this information quietly.

When this advantage was first introduced, I didn't think much of it. Perhaps I was too consumed in the challenge or my own thoughts then to really worry. But hearing it said again, like this, settles deep within my chest like a weight falling to the bottom of a pool. Whoever Valerie chooses has no say, regardless of what anyone else wants.

I force myself to breathe normally, not to panic over things that haven't happened yet, that are still to come, and that might not ever occur.

"Ladies," Miranda continues, "when I call your name, you'll share your reason for your decision before revealing your choice. The floor will be yours, so be honest." A small smile forms on her face.

With a nod, the ceremony begins, starting with a name draw. Jessa is called first. She steps forward.

"Jessa, please reveal your choice." Miranda gestures.

"This person, since being here, has given me some perspective on the world. They've made me laugh in a way I don't think I have in a long time. And this choice I'm making feels the easiest. Right. So I choose..." She pauses. "Nick," she says with a smile before walking calmly toward him. They share a kiss as he holds her tight.

But I don't pay much attention.

My mind wanders again to last night. Scott had sounded certain. That low, direct voice in the half dark. Every word seemed sincere, genuine, like it was simply a fact he was tired of keeping to himself. And I had stood there at the bathroom counter, working very hard to not let him and his words enchant me. At least not too much. The desire to believe him while still holding on to the reality that the other shoe could drop at any moment is a balance as challenging as walking on a tight rope.

Please don't have me be the fool.

My pulse kicks up with each selection. Ava picks Zayne with a smug smile to Kylie. Surprisingly, Kylie chooses Sean. And even more shocking Renee selects Bradley.

How much of what they're saying in their testimonial is true? Even if there is some truth to their words, how long would that truth be genuine? This time only lasts for ten days, and we've already gone through a week of it.

Then there are three men left: Trevor, Damon, and Scott. Only Emily, Valerie, and I remain.

Miranda calls another name. "Emily."

When this started, I was glad to have time to breathe before the inevitable choice I know I'll have to make. I hoped I could use that time to finalize a decision. But now I realize I haven't made one, turning this time into torture.

I don't know what to do.

Emily steps forward. I watch her scan all around her, not just at the three men in front of her. She looks as nervous as I feel.

Giving a heartfelt statement, she finally calls Trevor's name. And with a relieved smile, she walks over to his waiting arms.

Then Valerie steps forward. Her blue sundress flows in the wind, her hair loose around her shoulders. She seems cool and collected. Not like she doesn't care about the outcome, but rather like someone who has made her decision and settled it. She takes a breath, hands loosely clasped.

"I came into this experience thinking I knew exactly what I wanted," she begins, her voice warm and measured. "Someone ready. Someone uncomplicated. What I found instead surprised me." She pauses. "I found someone who reminded me what it actually feels like to be in the presence of a real man. Someone grounded in a way most people here aren't. Someone I think deserves to be chosen."

Her vague words have my nerves skittering.

My eyes move to Scott, searching for any kind of reaction, anything that would give me a hint of an answer. But he's gone quiet. Not in his usual stillness, but something tighter underneath it—the look of a man hearing something he wasn't expecting, jaw locked, shoulders rigid, like the ground just shifted under his feet while the cameras keep rolling.

He has no idea what's going on, either.

He looks alarmed.

Why?

Neither of us know what's about to happen. And that fear I'd tried to bury claws its way back up, sharper than before.

"My choice," Valerie says, her eyes moving between the two men as if she were standing on a great precipice and about to jump—taking someone with her in the process, "is Scott."

The name settles like ice into the morning air.

Around me, the group reacts. Murmurs ripple; a few gasps cut through the breeze.

I freeze in place. I can't move.

Valerie crosses the terrace with easy, unhurried confidence. When she reaches Scott, she rises onto her toes and presses a kiss to his cheek, her hand curling around his arm, settling beside him. He remains as rigid as before. His expression panicked, his eyes erratic like he's working something over in his mind at lightspeed. Then his gaze snaps straight to me.

Was what he said last night a lie? Or was he telling the truth… and this blindsided him, too? The questions slam into me so hard my stomach twists. I harden my expression, force my face into blank calm, and look away.

I feel Scott's eyes on me. I don't give him the satisfaction of meeting them again. Instead, I straighten and turn my gaze to Damon.

Moments later, Miranda calls me to stand beside Damon. I'm grateful that this is finally over.

Emily's hand finds mine at my side. Quiet. Discreet. Just there.

Behind me somewhere Scott is standing next to Valerie with her hand still on his arm.

I turn away, not looking back as I grip Emily's hand.

But the confusion doesn't leave. It only grows—thick, heavy, more tangled than ever.

~

Day 7 (Late Morning/Afternoon)

Scott

Miranda steps forward before anyone even gets a chance to breathe.

"Before everyone disperses," she says, clapping her hands together with that fake smile she saves for shitstorms, "one more update. Starting tonight, we're moving to co-ed sleeping arrangements."

The group loses their minds. Voices overlap, Kylie mutters a curse under her breath, and a producer in the back just nods like it's Tuesday.

Miranda continues. "You'll have the afternoon to get settled. New couples, my suggestion is to use the time to get to know each other better because soon you'll be sharing a bed."

Suggestion, my ass.

I lock my face down, eyes straight ahead. My brain's already spinning.

What the actual fuck just happened?

I told Valerie flat-out I wasn't interested, suggested she should pick

Damon. Why the hell would she choose me anyway? Why throw away her advantage like that? Unless she doesn't see it that way.

This is a goddamn cluster fuck. On one side, I've got a woman I don't want thinking we're a thing. On the other, Lyla's about to get hauled off by Damon, and I can't stop it. And even if I did, regardless of cameras, I don't think she'd let me.

I need to know why Valerie chose me. Before this day gets any worse.

I grab Valerie's arm, gentle but firm. "We need to talk."

She doesn't fight it, following me through the scattering crowd.

The villa's already turning into chaos—bags hitting floors, people claiming beds, that low hum of everyone figuring out the new rules. I don't stop. I've had this spot mapped since day one. A narrow gap between the kitchen and the production hallway where the two corner cameras don't quite overlap. A blind spot.

I steer us in, looking back behind me to make sure we're not being followed, and put my back against the wall. I then reach down and kill my mic pack. She must realize what I'm doing because then she does the same with hers. We've got maybe thirty seconds before production notices they can't see or hear us. It's not ideal, but it's what I've got.

"Why did you do that?" I ask, keeping my voice low.

Valerie's composure cracks. Tears well in her eyes.

"I'm not mad," I tell her. On the outside, I'm calm. Inside, I'm already calculating how fast this is going to blow up in my face. "Just tell me what happened."

She swallows hard. "I was going to pick Damon. I'd decided last night after dinner. But this morning, right before the ceremony, a producer pulled me aside."

My stomach drops. I already have an inkling on where this is going.

"She sat me down. Said she'd been watching the footage from our date. Told me she saw something real between us." Valerie's voice wavers. "She asked why I was so quick to throw it away just to play it safe."

I go completely still.

These motherfuckers.

They know exactly which buttons to push.

Valerie keeps going, words tumbling out. "She made it sound like choosing you was the brave thing. Like picking Damon was me running away from something good again. Same crap I always do. She got in my head, Scott. By the time I was standing there, I...I just said your name. I didn't realize what I'd done until it was out. I'm so sorry."

I can't be pissed at her. Not really. She's just another person this show is chewing up and spitting back out. They manipulate scenarios and emotions for a living. She never stood a chance.

"It's not your fault," I say. The words taste like ash.

But the real problem hits me like a gut punch.

Lyla is never going to believe a word I say now. Not after this. Not with us split up, not with cameras in every corner, not with Damon right there for Lyla to think she'd be better off with him. I can explain until I'm blue in the face, and I worry it won't matter. This place is rigged. I've known that for a while. But now that it's royally screwed us like this, every move I make will only give her another reason to think I'm full of shit.

Valerie wipes at her cheek. "For what it's worth...I saw her face when I said your name. She's not as indifferent as she's pretending."

I don't answer. Because that's the worst part. Even if she's hurting, even if some tiny part of her still wants what we had, I've got no way to come off as genuine. Not here. Not like this.

I answer with a plastered-on smile. "Thank you, Valerie."

I click my mic back on, gesturing to her with a nod that she should do the same, and step out of the blind spot like the conversation never happened.

The afternoon drags in that slow, forced way the show loves—meals, small talk, everyone pretending this new coed bullshit is normal. By evening, the novelty's worn off and everyone is simply tired.

I keep eyes on Lyla the whole time. She sticks close to Emily, laughing when she's supposed to, nodding at the right spots. A perfect performance. But I know her. She's confused, spiraling. And right now I'm probably the last person on earth she wants anywhere near her.

The shared room, designed barrack style, fills up as night rolls in. Seven beds in two rows on opposite sides facing each other, ceiling fans turn lazily, ocean rumbling through the louvered windows. Everyone begins to settle into the awkward dynamic no one asked for.

Out of habit, I take the bed nearest the window on the left. My back to the wall, with a clear line to the door. Valerie climbs in on the other side of the bed without a word. We just exist next to each other like two people who already said everything that needed saying.

Those fucking producers. Manipulating Valerie like that, finding the exact crack in her head, twisting until picking me sounded like the brave choice instead of the safe one. Misinformation getting to Lyla before I even finished dinner. The challenge that paired me with Valerie in the first place, handing her the advantage without realizing it'd kick off this whole chain reaction.

The lights drop to almost nothing.

I look across and see Lyla in the bed third from the left. On her side, she faces away, her hair loose on the pillow. Her shoulders seem tight, like she's forcing herself to stay still. She's wide awake and pretending she's not. The same way she was at seventeen when she didn't want anyone to see her break.

Their corner goes dark.

I stare back up at the ceiling again. She's ten feet away, and I can't say a fucking word. Not without the whole room being in on it. Not without production catching it and giving them ammunition to make things worse.

I can't win in here.

The thought hits hard and sticks. Staying won't change shit. Even if I somehow get her to talk to me again, the show will just keep twisting things. Producers will poke another crack, and cameras will catch whatever they need for ratings and spin it. I'm willing to eat all this bullshit for her, but right now, it feels like using a stationary bike as transportation. It doesn't prove a damn thing.

She needs something this place can't give her.

And so do I.

Only one move comes to mind. One thing they can't redirect or reframe if I do it just right. One gesture that's completely mine and irreversible. I'd be risking everything doing this, but what choice do I have?

I need to leave.

Chapter Eighteen

Day Eight

Lyla

I register the consuming warmth beside me before my eyes are even open.

Another body's familiar weight. The slow, even rhythm of breathing that isn't mine. The particular slant of morning light slicing through the windows. For one unguarded heartbeat, suspended between sleep and waking, I almost let myself sink into that warmth—

Then reality crashes in. Yesterday's debacle. The ceremony, watching Scott climb into bed, then lay beside Valerie until the lights went out.

I snap open my eyes.

Damon lies with his back facing me, his breathing slow and even in the deep, untroubled sleep of a man that has nothing left unresolved. I watch the steady rhythm too long, and the old hollow in my chest cracks wider, goes deeper than before, raw and gnawing, like teeth working bone from the inside.

Nothing about this feels right.

I turn my head. Across the room, Scott is already awake. Flat on his back, one arm cocked behind his head, eyes fixed on the ceiling like he's been mapping every crack for hours. Valerie sleeps deeply on the far side of the mattress, as though she tried not to touch him.

He must sense I'm awake because he turns his head in my direction. Our gazes lock across the distance.

Nothing moves except the lazy spin of the ceiling fan. Outside, the ocean exhales against the shore. That familiar pull to him ignites in my chest.

Damn him.

After yesterday, after Valerie chose him, how can he still look at me like that? Is there more to the story, or does he think he can have his cake and eat it, too?

I break first, sliding out of bed, and being careful not to disturb the sheets still warm from Damon's body. I reach for my cardigan on the nightstand, pull it on, and pad toward the bathroom without looking back.

The morning unfolds the way morning on this island has since day one—coffee, fruit, the low hum of half-awake voices.

I claim the chair beside Emily, curl both hands around my mug, and let the group's chatter wash over me like white noise.

I'm halfway through my second cup when I hear familiar footsteps behind me.

"Can I talk to you for a minute?"

Scott's voice echoes in my ears, sliding under my skin like it always does, low and steady. He stops beside my chair, holding a glass bowl of granola and yogurt. He sets it in front of me like an offering, then waits.

I set my mug down beside the bowl. "Scott—"

"Not here." He angles his head toward the far side of the pool deck where the morning shade still clings and the nearest camera is twenty feet away. "Just for a minute."

I sigh. If I don't go now, he'll keep asking me until I do.

Standing, I follow. The space between us stays careful, deliberate, like we're both afraid one wrong step will ignite whatever's still smoldering from yesterday.

What else could he have to say other than what I already know? That doesn't change the strain between us.

When we reach the quieter end of the deck, I turn to face him, arms crossed. "Go ahead."

He studies me for a long beat, blue eyes scanning like he's reading every line I haven't spoken. Whatever he sees makes him tighten his jaw before he smooths it away.

"I know you don't want to hear this," he starts, voice rough. "But what happened yesterday wasn't—"

"Scott." The word comes out flat, tired. Last night I felt confusion and heartache. Now I just feel numb. "I already know what you're going to say. And I'm not going to call you a liar. For all I know, you could be telling the truth. But I will never know that for certain. I don't care if it was real or scripted or whatever the hell it was between you and Valerie yesterday. None of matters to me anymore."

His expression shifts. Jaw flexing. "How does it not matter—"

"Because it doesn't," I reply plainly, flat and final. Yesterday still sits heavy in my chest like a stone I can't swallow, but I refuse to let it drag me under again. I have to choose me. I can't keep pining for a man I'm not sure I can trust with my heart—or my body. "I've said it before, but I mean it this time. I can't keep doing this. I can't keep letting myself want you when I don't know if any of what you say is real."

I pause, the truth scraping raw on its way out. "We both just need to move forward. Whatever that looks like."

"Not with me?"

Silence falls between us, thick and electric. The ocean keeps its steady rhythm behind us, but everything else holds still.

He looks at me solemnly, those blue eyes reading every flicker I'm trying to hide. "Is there anything I can do to change your mind?"

I sigh, the sound too heavy for the morning air. "I don't know what to think or trust anymore."

He holds my gaze. I meet it. We stare at each other like this for a long, aching moment. The part of me I've been locking down, the traitorous one that still remembers his hands and his mouth and the way his voice used to say my name like it belonged to him, almost wishes he'd reach for me. Just once. Just enough to make me break. To change my mind.

But he doesn't.

"Okay," he says quietly. No fight. No push. He simply nods, turns, and walks away.

I should feel better about this.

I don't. Instead, I feel like a huge hole has been punched through my chest.

I head back across the deck toward the table. Emily is watching me over the rim of her coffee cup. That careful expression on her face that says she's debating whether to ask.

I shake my head once.

She nods, understanding.

Dropping into my chair, I pick up the bowl of granola and yogurt Scott left me and start eating. My coffee has gone cold, but I don't care. This food is the only thing that seems to comfort me now.

The morning stretches into afternoon, and I move through the day on autopilot, smile glued in place, heart somewhere back on the shaded deck with the man who finally stopped chasing me.

I grab a water from the bar when Emily falls into step beside me.

Touching my shoulder, she holds my gaze. I stare back in confusion. She doesn't say anything at first. Then—

"I need to show you something." She scans around her as though careful about who could be watching.

"What?"

She glances once toward the nearest camera mounted above the corridor junction, then back to me. "Follow me."

She leads me through the common area and into a narrow gap between the kitchen and the production hallway.

What does she want me to see? The pantry?

I've never had a reason to meander over here. But I quickly realize that I probably should have. It's quiet with the ambient hum of production equipment somewhere behind a thick wall and the distant sound of the ocean.

Emily pulls me into a corner, and I realize then why she has me in this particular spot. This is a blind spot in the cameras.

I open my mouth to speak.

She shakes her head, standing beside me before reaching behind her and clicking off her mic. She gestures for me to do the same.

"Why?" I mouth.

She reaches into the pocket of her shorts, producing an envelope with my name written on the front—in Scott's handwriting.

My heart pounds in my chest as I click off my mic, too.

What the hell is going on? Why is Emily handing me an envelope with Scott's handwriting on it? Couldn't he have handed it to me himself? Now that I think about it, I haven't seen him since this morning.

"He asked me to give it to you and for you to read it alone."

Giving me a compassionate smile, she reaches behind her again and clicks her mic back on before walking away.

I stand in the quiet for a moment, looking at my name. The envelope is sealed. And whatever is inside has weight, like there's more than paper inside.

Why should I open this?

On the one hand, I have every reason not to. This little thing doesn't erase the past, much less make what happened yesterday go away.

But then there's the what-if questions that go off in my mind. What if I don't open it and something happens? What if I do open it and it means nothing?

What if I do open it, and it changes everything?

In the end, curiosity wins and I open the letter.

Inside is a single written page and a picture of a small, one-story starter home with blue shutters. The property looks like it's on the edge of open land, modest and quiet. The house has a covered porch facing a lake. It looks like somewhere a person could breathe. Somewhere they could build a life.

What is this?

I read the letter:

Lyla,

I've never been good at saying the right thing at the

right time. You know that better than anyone. So I'm writing this down because if I tried to say it to your face, you'd find a way to stop me before I finished, and I need you to hear all of it.

I came here for you. Only you. From the moment I found out you'd be on this show, there was never a question in my mind about whether I'd follow. I would have found my way back to you eventually. This just gave me a reason to stop waiting.

I need you to know that nothing happened with Valerie. Not at dinner, not after. She's a good woman who deserves to find what she's looking for. But she never was for me. Nobody here is. Nobody anywhere has been, for ten years, and I'm done pretending that's something I can change by staying in a place that keeps turning every honest thing between us into a story it can use.

I know you don't trust me. That you may never trust me. I know I haven't earned it. And I know that staying here and enduring two more days of challenges and cameras and whatever the producers engineer next won't change that. It'll only give you more reasons to doubt what's real and what isn't. I can't win you back inside this place. I've come to realize that. All this time, I thought leaving was like giving up.

But now I know it's the only honest thing I have left to give you. So this is me giving it.

I'm not asking you to forgive ten years overnight. I'm not asking you to trust me because I wrote it in a letter. I'm asking you to consider the possibility that what we had was real, that what we found again here was real, and that the man waiting for you on the other side of this is not the boy who left.

Several years ago, when I didn't know how or when I

could find my way back to you, I bought this house that you see in the photo. I bought it for when I could come back to you. So we could truly start our lives together. It's been sitting empty ever since.

Now it doesn't have to anymore. You'll soon understand.

I look down at the small photograph in my hands. What does he mean by *anymore*? That I'll *soon understand*?

Come find me here when you're ready. Or don't. But know that I'll be there either way.

Whatever you decide, I will always love you, little one.

Yours forever and always,

Scott.

I read it again. Three times. Four.

Each time slower than the last, like slowing down would help me absorb what the words are actually saying.

Why am I getting this? Why send an address when he's here at the villa?

I still. This isn't just a love letter. It's goodbye.

I have to find him.

I fold the letter carefully back into the envelope, tucking the photograph against it. And I rush out of the gap and back into the common area.

I scan the area. He isn't in the common room. Not on the pool deck, the beach, or even the gym.

He bought a house for us, even when he didn't know if there was a guarantee we'd be with each other again. And he held on to it for ten years. That's not the man I thought he was. Far from it.

Which would make everything about Valerie true, too.

I run into the bedroom to find his belongings alongside his bed gone.

I can't find him. He's not here anymore.

The weight of that letter finally hits me, crashing through every wall I spent so long rebuilding. He didn't just say he'd choose me. He left to prove it. He walked away from this show—from the cameras, the competition, from whatever the producers wanted from him—and he did it not to punish or pressure me but to hand the choice back to me entirely. All this time, I've been wondering if I should trust him with my heart again, when I've known the answer all along.

And he put our future in my hands— What have I done?

Anger at myself flares within me. Those things I said to him this morning come back to my mind. I was so convinced I already knew how this ended. So convinced that protecting myself was the same thing as being right. So convinced that I was better off. But I was wrong.

He said to meet him somewhere. But where?

I dig back into the envelope, fishing out the picture, and turn it over. On the back is Scott's handwriting of an address in black ink. It's back in Dallas, local—not far.

I have to go after him. But how? That penalty clause is six-figures I don't have. How can I convince them to let me go without breaking the bank? I could sneak off, but I don't know the first thing about driving a boat. And it's not like I can swim. Regardless, I have to try.

The shared bedroom is dead quiet when I start yanking my things out of the nightstand and closet, shoving them into my suitcase. Everyone else is still outside at the group dinner, which is exactly what I need—ten minutes alone to pack without an audience and without having to explain myself to anyone before I'm ready.

My hands move on autopilot. Clothes, toiletries, charger, everything crammed in fast and messy. Organization and folding are out the window.

I drop onto the edge of the bed and exhale a breath I didn't realize I'd been holding.

The door clicks open.

One of the female producers steps in—sharp eyes, tablet in hand, the kind of calm that says she's seen everything and is forever unfazed by even the most outrageous meltdowns. Her gaze flicks from my face to the suitcase and back.

"Everything okay, Lyla? You look like you're about to bolt. What's going on?"

I stand up fast. "Glad you're here. I need to leave the villa. Right now."

Her brow lifts slightly. "Okay, I get you. But you know the clause is two hundred—"

"I know." I nod. "I'd like to negotiate. There're only two days left. Let me pay for those days, and I can do an exit interview, give you whatever exclusive you need for the finale, whatever it takes. Just process the paperwork."

She doesn't blink. "Actually, that's what I wanted to talk to you about. It's already been taken care of."

I stop cold.

"The penalty," she continues matter-of-factly. "We received instructions this morning to process your exit. Scott arranged to lease out a property of his to cover your clause, while he paid his penalty in full."

The room goes very still.

"He what?"

"You're free to leave whenever you're ready."

I stare at her. She stares back with that professional blank face that says she's delivered worse news and knows better than to fill the silence.

Lease out a property? Could she mean…

It's been sitting empty ever since. Now it doesn't have to anymore.

I reach into the envelope and pull out the photograph. The small house in the photo in his letter. Is that what she meant? But why would he do that?

For me. He did it for me.

I feel my throat close, tears blur my vision.

"Thank you," I manage.

"Come to the dock with your luggage when you're ready." She steps out, pulling the door closed behind her.

I tuck the photograph back into the envelope and finish packing.

I'm zipping the suitcase when the door opens again. I look up.

Damon steps inside, looking at me—the suitcase, my expression, the envelope on top of my clothes—before turning his gaze back on me. He doesn't look surprised. In fact, he looks relieved.

He closes the door behind him.

"Hey," he says.

"Hey." I straighten. "I see Emily told you where I was."

Before I left dinner early to pack, I asked Emily to tell Damon where to find me. I hate that I'm doing this now, but he deserves the truth, a proper goodbye.

"Yeah. Everything okay?"

"Great. Better than it has been in a while."

"I'm guessing your filled suitcase has something to do with that."

I nod. "I'm leaving."

"I've gathered that." He pauses, as if he's just realized something. "You're going after him." He moves to the edge of the bed across from mine and sits, forearms on his knees, unhurried. "I've been watching you all day. All week, if I'm being honest."

I meet his eyes. "I'm sorry, Damon."

"Don't be," he replies earnestly. "I'm not."

"I should have been clearer with myself sooner. With you."

He shakes his head. "You were figuring it out. I understand. When are you leaving?"

"Now," I reply.

He nods slowly, looking down at his hands for a second before looking back up. "Then in that case, can I tell you something?"

"Please."

"I knew it wasn't going to be me." He chuckles lightly. "The way you went still when he walked into any room. The way you froze at that ceremony. I kept telling myself maybe compatibility was enough, that maybe you just needed time to adjust." He exhales. "But then I realized you need more than what I can give you."

My chest tightens for him as I sit beside him. "You deserve more than something safe. You deserve happiness, too."

He gives a small, tired smile. "Sweet of you. But that ship sailed a long time ago."

He reaches over and takes my hand for a second, steady and warm.

"You need someone who makes you feel everything. Not someone who makes things easy. And watching you try to settle for easy..." He shakes his head. "That's not you. Never was. I see that now."

He stands, pulls me into a quick, solid hug, then lets go.

When he steps back, his face is calm. Decided.

"Now, go get him," he says. "before he does something sensible like move on."

I laugh at his facetious joke as my eyes sting.

I start for the door, then stop. "Damon?"

"Yeah?"

I turn back. "I meant what I said."

He smiles then. A genuine smile I haven't seen since we met. "Maybe so." He picks up the handle of my suitcase and hands it to me. "You know...I've always wanted to visit Dallas."

"Hope to hear from you soon then." I return the smile.

I take the bag, tuck the envelope under my arm, and walk out the door.

Chapter Nineteen

Lyla

After landing on the red-eye at Dallas-Fort Worth the next morning, the address takes me forty minutes south by Uber.

For the plane ride, I was a nervous wreck. Being in the Uber, I'm even worse. The sooner I get there, the better.

I spend most of the car ride with the envelope in my lap and the photograph face-up on top of it, watching the city give way to quieter roads and wider skies—and trying not to think too hard about what I'm going to say when I get there.

But what *do* I say? *Scott, I know I told you to fuck off, but I was wrong. I love you.*

Oh, god, that's awful.

I've always been the woman who prepares every word before she speaks. I built a business on planning ahead, knowing exactly what to say and when to say it. And right now, heading toward a small house on the outskirts of town, with a photograph in my hand and ten years of unfinished business, my mind is too muddled to think straight.

Not too long ago, I was ready to leave all my deepest emotions and desires in the past. Ready to live a life with someone safe and compatible rather than someone I burned for and deeply still loved. I thought that would be enough. Now I know, as I head toward the man I know I can't live without, I couldn't have been more wrong.

I'm scared out of my mind. What if this doesn't work out? What if he changes his mind? All the what-ifs scroll through my mind. I have about a million reasons to have the driver turn around and head for my apartment instead. But I only have one good one that's keeping me moving forward.

I don't know what the future holds, but I know I'd rather not live it without him.

The Uber slows at the edge of the property. The house sits just on top of a small hill.

There it is.

It looks exactly like the photograph—modest, quiet, a covered porch facing a large lake and open land beside it, with the last of the early morning light catching the windows and turning them gold. A black truck is parked in the driveway.

He's there. He has to be.

When the driver stops, I climb out and stare at the place before me.

A part of me tells me I should wait, think this through. I don't know what I'm going to walk into. But the pit in my stomach tells me to move.

I've had ten years of being cautious alone. Now all I see is him.

I stand there for about three seconds, luggage in hand, before every instinct overrides every last bit of thought.

At first, I walk, then move faster. Next thing I know, I'm running across the open ground toward the front door. Even though I'm running faster than I ever have in my life, I still feel like I can't get there fast enough.

The front door isn't locked when I reach for the door handle.

With no hesitation, I push it open and rush inside.

The house is stark as I walk farther in, closing the door behind me. No pictures. A kitchen with gray countertops and white backsplash is to my left. There's no other furniture in sight.

"Scott—" I call him. "Scott."

He appears from an empty space to my right, wearing a plain white T-shirt and jeans. He looks relieved to see me.

I freeze in place. My pulse jumps. He's here—in front of me. And this moment is just for us. No cameras or producers in sight. It's the first time in ten years a point in time truly belongs to us.

He stops, too.

We look at each other from opposite ends of the hallway. The house is quiet around us. No production hum, no carefully engineered atmosphere. Just me, just him, and the irreducible fact that it's only us.

I close the distance first. No more running. No more second guessing. All I want, all I need, is him.

I stop just in front of him, only a few feet apart. I'm close enough that I have to tilt my face up to look at him properly. He towers over me as he looks down. His body heat radiates onto me.

For a moment, neither of us says a word. He doesn't touch me, doesn't try to come any closer. He looks as though he's waiting. As if he's trying to process that I'm standing right in front of him.

"I don't know how to want you without the fear of losing you," I say finally, my voice quiet but steady. "That's the honest truth that I've been carrying since the first day you walked into that villa."

He remains perfectly still, listening.

I continue. "I know I shut you down. Not just yesterday morning but also plenty of times before that. But you never gave up. Not once." My throat tightens. "I'm not here because I've stopped being afraid. I haven't. I'm here because I read your letter, saw that photograph, and realized I'd rather be terrified with you than safe without you. That's the scariest decision I've ever made. But I trust it. I want to trust you."

Something shifts across his face, slow and complete. Like a door opening from the inside that had been locked for so long.

"You came," he says, rough.

"I came."

"Then you know." He steps closer, voice dropping low as he lifts one hand to cup my cheek. "You have to know I did all of it for you."

"I know." I exhale with a shaky breath. "I know that now."

His fingers trace my jaw, soft and light, as if he were mapping out my face for the first time. I close my eyes, letting the simmering heat of his touch sink straight into my bones.

"I don't know what happens next," I whisper.

"That's okay." His forehead drops to mine. "We're together. That's what matters."

"I don't know how to do this without waiting for the other shoe to drop."

"You don't have to control it." His breath brushes my lips. "You just have to stop running from it."

I open my eyes.

He's right there—across a decade of silence, one impossible island, forty minutes in an Uber with the photograph burning in my lap, and now this quiet house he bought when he was still a boy who believed in forever.

"I love you," I say, because it's true, and it's always been true. "And I don't think I ever stopped."

His exhale is slow, shaky in a way I've never heard from him before—like he's been holding that breath since he was eighteen.

"I love you, too," he murmurs. "I never stopped, either, little one."

He pulls me in—one strong arm around my back, the other threading deep into my hair—and I willingly lean in. When his mouth finally meets mine, the kiss is slow at first, almost reverent, like he's afraid I'll disappear. Then I open for him, and everything ignites. His tongue slides against mine, hungry and claiming, a low groan vibrating from his chest straight into mine. Ten years of silence, fear, and want pour out in the taste of him: salt, spice, and home. My body melts against his like it was always meant to.

When we finally break apart, we're breathless, trembling. The fear is still there...but so am I.

Right here.

With him.

Epilogue

Six Months later

Scott

The ballroom smells of gardenias and candlelight.

I pull Lyla close to me, her hand folding in mine and head tucked just below my jaw as we sway to the rhythm of the slow music. I take in her scent of vanilla and something definitely her.

"Scott, I'm working."

"Humor me for just this song." I nuzzle her neck. Around us, two hundred guests exist in their own orbits.

Six months ago, I stood in our house and watched her come through the door. A sight I only dreamed of seeing.

Three months ago, we watched the fiasco that was The One That Got Away in our small living room. We were ecstatic to find out Emily and Zayne not only started a relationship together shortly after we left despite the coupling ceremony, but they also had won the one hundred thousand dollars.

Four weeks ago, she stood in a white dress next to me in a Dallas courthouse as we made our promises of forever and said *I do* like it was the simplest decision we've ever made. And ever since, I couldn't be happier.

Lyla's fingers lace through mine.

I would have married her anywhere. Hell, I would have married her in the parking lot if she'd asked.

"You okay?" Her voice is warm and low against my neck.

"Fantastic."

She tilts her head back just far enough to look at me. The purple silk of her dress catches the string lights overhead, and the gold band on her ring finger catches everything else. Her eyes stare softly into mine. Unguarded. Certain.

"Still the most beautiful thing I've ever seen," I whisper to her.

She blushes. One of my favorite reactions from her—a close second to her moans.

"How on earth did we get here?"

The corner of my mouth curves. "Should I tell the scenic version?"

She laughs as I pull her a half-step closer.

The string quartet somewhere behind us shifts into something slower. The gardenias mingle with faint champagne and the warm Texas night, drifting through the open floor-to-ceiling windows. Somewhere down the corridor, muffled by two sets of closed doors, a processional is just getting underway. The venue is running two events tonight, another couple in the east wing still at the altar. Around us, dinner conversation, glasses clinking, the low hum of a reception functioning exactly the way it should. I don't hear any of it. Only Lyla's even breathing, slowing to match mine. I have her completely relaxed in my arms.

Beyond Lyla and the dance floor, I notice Damon.

A few weeks ago, he popped in for a visit and has been spending time here ever since. He's actually become a good friend.

"Do you think Damon will continue to stay in town?"

Lyla turns her head in Damon's direction. "Hope so. I think Dallas is growing on him."

Damon stands near one of the large windows, slightly apart from the nearest cluster of guests. He wears a meticulous charcoal suit, not a thread out of place. A glass of scotch sits on the high-top beside him. Untouched.

As if he senses eyes on him, his gaze cuts across the room and finds Lyla and me.

He nods once with a small smile.

I give him the same.

Then he walks toward us, tapping Lyla on the shoulder. "I'm going to head out. Thanks for letting me watch you work. It was a lot of fun."

She beams. "Happy for you to join us. Let's get together next week."

"You bet. And my treat this time, Bennett." he says as he moves toward the valet doors, waving with one hand and burying the other in his pants pocket.

"He's leaving early," Lyla murmurs against my shoulder, eyes tracking the movement.

"You know how he is. This isn't exactly his scene. And...let's be honest, he's a bit of a workaholic."

She nods in agreement. "Very true. You think he'll find someone worth staying permanently for?"

"Don't know. Guess time will tell." I press my lips to her hair as we keep dancing. "But he might have a point about leaving. How soon can I get you back into our bed, wife?"

She giggles. "Soon, husband. Soon."

The string quartet fades under a wave of laughter and clinking glasses from the far end of the room. Outside, through the open windows, I catch the low purr of a black SUV engine idling at the valet line. Damon climbs behind the wheel and closes the driver's door behind him.

All of a sudden, gasps erupt to my left. And just as I turn my head, I see a flash of white silk bursting through the side doors at the far end of the entrance.

Lyla turns around to my line of sight, then goes still in my arms. "Oh, my god. Is she..."

"We got a runner!" someone yells, chasing the bride. Not far behind, a burly man runs like his life depends on it.

"Isabelle, wait."

But Isabelle doesn't seem to listen as she hikes her gown without breaking stride, moving fast across the hallway like a woman who has already made up her mind.

The bride makes quick work as she escapes the building through the valet—and toward Damon's car.

Why is she getting in his car? Does she know him? Is something going on?

Questions swirl, not just in my mind but no doubt in this entire room as we watch her climb into his SUV, closing the door behind her. The car sits idle at the valet line. Through the windshield, I watch the moment Damon sees her—the exact second headlights from an arriving car catch her face and she catches his. Neither of them move. A moment seems to pass between them. Then two.

She says something to him with an urgent look on her face.

Damon doesn't seem to flinch because then he shifts into gear and the SUV pulls away, tires biting gravel with a sharp crunch that carries above the noise of the reception.

"Isabelle, no. Come back, you stupid girl." The burly man's voice explodes in the middle of the road where the car was moments before. He leans over in exhaustion, hands on his knees. I make the safe assumption that's the father of the bride, given his age and attire.

Lyla's hand tightens in mine behind her back before pulling back just enough to look up at me. Half stunned, half like she might laugh in disbelief.

"Did that just—"

"Yep," I reply.

"Should we—"

"Let him figure things out on his own." I pull her back into my arms, filing the intense moment away.

She nods, melting into me with ease. "You're right."

"Dance with me, Mrs. Bennett."

"With pleasure, Mr. Bennett."

So we do.

The ballroom hums with easy conversation and music again moments later.

Only two things are on my mind now: Lyla and the long life ahead of us.

I ran away from my wedding...and straight into the arms of my enemy.

HOW TO BREAK A BAD BOY
The How-To Series, Book 6
by Mallory Black
(will be available in eBook and print)

Join my newsletter at MalloryBlack.com now to be the first to know all the things. You'll be the first to know about new releases, sales, give-aways, and exclusive content, including cover reveals. Don't miss any of the fun!

For signed copies of my books and more, check out the Shayla Store at ShaylaBlackStore.com!

Loved HOW TO SEDUCE THE EX? Help spread the word by reviewing and sharing with your book-loving besties. Your support means the world to me!

Books by Mallory Black

CONTEMPORARY ROMANCE

THE HOW TO SERIES

Sexy, Sassy, Witty Romance

How to One-Night Stand (Kiera & Jonathan)

How to Fake a Fiancé (Kami & Ian)

How to Marry the Boss (Jake & Mia)

How to Play the Player (Nathan & Quinn)

How to Seduce the Ex (Scott & Lyla)

How to Break a Bad Boy

About Mallory Black

Mallory Black is the author of sassy, sexy contemporary romances with happily-ever-afters.

In middle school, Mallory discovered the joy of reading and started devouring books of all kinds. But as the only child of the New York Times and USA Today bestselling romance author Shayla Black, Mallory grew up with romance publishing. In college, she began her own love affair with the romance writing world and, with her degree in English/Writing from TCU in 2022, decided to pursue a publishing career and embrace her love of storytelling.

Mallory currently lives in North Texas with her incredibly supportive parents and two silly, spoiled tabbies. When she's not spinning stories in her head, she enjoys reading, hanging out with her boyfriend, listening to music, and spending time with family.

Connect with Mallory online:

Newsletter: http://eepurl.com/hWG2xT
Website: https://malloryblack.com
Facebook Reader Group

facebook.com/mallory.black.79274

instagram.com/malloryblackauthor

tiktok.com/@malloryblackauthor

goodreads.com/malloryblack

bookbub.com/profile/1282562347

amazon.com/stores/Mallory-Black/author/B0BPGZFTHT

www.ingramcontent.com/pod-product-compliance
Lightning Source LLC
LaVergne TN
LVHW010659110826
845149LV00014B/3162

* 9 7 8 1 9 5 9 0 6 5 0 9 8 *